Descansos

Words from the Wayside

More From Darkhouse Books

Descansos
Words from the Wayside

Susannah Carlson, Editor
Wulf Losee, Poetry Editor

DARKHOUSE BOOKS

Niles, California

Descansos
Words From the Wayside

Anthology copyright © 2017 by Darkhouse Books
ISBN 978-1-945467-00-4
Published June 2017
Published in the United States of America

Shrine Stories ©2017 Jesse Sensibar ▲ Thebes—The Coming of War ©2017 Terence Kuch ▲ I'll Go Now ©2017 Cate McGowan ▲ Thirteen ©2017 Armine Mortimer ▲ Foota Forever ©2017 Tyson West ▲ Monuments of Absence ©2017 Richard King Perkins II ▲ Living the Dream ©2011 Terresa Cooper Haskew. Previously published in *Altered States*. (*Main Street Rag*, 2011) ▲ Flying ©2017 D. Dina Friedman ▲ The Road to Paihia ©2017 Frank Russo. Previously published in *In the Museum of Creation*. ▲ After Your Husband Dies – An Instruction Manual ©2017 Amber Colleen Hart ▲ A Song for the King ©2017 Brian Morgan ▲ Watermelon Baby ©2017 Ivan Faute. Previously published in *The Mochilla Review* (2008). ▲ The Best Revenge ©2007 Ellaraine Lockie Previously published in *Voices of Israel* (2007) and *Contrarywise: An Anthology* (2008). ▲ Angels of Mercy, Angels of Grief ©2002 Kurt Newton. Previously published in *Dark Demons* (2002). ▲ So Lonesome I Could Die ©2017 Jon Black ▲ Descanso for November 2016 ©2017 Lita Kurth ▲ New Mexico State Highway 76 ©2017 C.A. Cole. Previously published in *Moonsick Magazine* (2015). ▲ Burial at Fishkill Creek off I-84 ©2017 Kevin Wetmore ▲ My Blood Splatter Analysis of an Alcoholic's Excuse ©2017 Woody Woodger ▲ Tatort ©2017 Diana Brown ▲ Waiting by the Window ©2017 Jonathan Ochoco ▲ Tin-Tree Descanso ©2017 Teressa Rose Ezell ▲ The Tall Man ©2017 Nick Bouchard ▲ When You Least Expect it, a Jackrabbit ©2006 Fred Zackel. Previously published in *The Mississippi Review* (2006). ▲ Desesperanza ©2017 Dave Holt. An earlier version of this piece was published by Dog Ear Publishing, in *My Dreaming Waking Life*. ▲ Last Flight Out ©2017 Nicole Scherer. Previously published in *Air & Space/Smithsonian Magazine* (November 2016). ▲ Of Bees and Bumbling Men ©2017 Nancy Brewka-Clark ▲ A Guardrail ©2017 Jack Mackey ▲ 1968: A True Confession ©2015 John Z. Guzlowski ▲ Surviving Strangers ©2017 Scot Friesen ▲ Wayside Shrine ©2017 Pamela Ahlen ▲ Best Laid Plans ©2017 Mary Silwance ▲ Realist Flowers Sir Awake ©2017 Catherine A. Lee ▲ Mother Father Daughter ©2017 Hal Ackerman. Previously published in *I Wanna be Sedated*, and *Alfalfa* was published as a stand-alone in *Jewish Currents*. ▲ Negative Metaphor: My Dead Daughter's Lipstick ©2017 Jackie Davis Martin ▲ Like a Soul ©2013 Karen Bovenmyer. Previously published in *Stonecoast Review* (2013), *Creepy Campfire Quarterly* (2017), and *100 Voices Anthology* (2016). ▲ Anthology Copyright © 2017 Darkhouse Books ▲ Cover photo ©2017 Michele Wojcicki ▲ Cover & Book Design by Michele Wojcicki, type4udesign.com

Darkhouse Books • 160 J Street, #2223 • Niles, California 94536

TABLE OF CONTENTS

Introduction

Descansos, or roadside memorials, mark the place where a person's intended trajectory unexpectedly ended. They bear witness and speak honestly of the grief of those left behind, while reminding us as we hurtle past that we could meet the same fate just around the next bend. Descansos span cultures and centuries, and carry an immediacy and intimacy one doesn't feel in cemeteries. They take myriad shapes, from simple crosses to ornate shrines, from a teddy bear tied to a tree to a shattered helmet nailed to a fence.

This is a different kind of anthology. One bound together solely by the descanso, regardless of genre or form. The poetry, flash fiction, essays, and short stories contained within are as varied as the memorials that thematically unite them. From San Francisco to New Zealand to Greece, from a Navy pilot retiring to her helicopter to a musician in small town Texas whose life has just begun, from a woman taking supplies to the Water Protectors at Standing Rock, to the frightening fate of roadkill that take too long to die, these pieces reflect their authors' unique takes on themes of grief and love and sudden redirection.

Between these pages you will find poetry and prose that runs the gamut from literary to political; from science fiction to horror to ghost stories. Reading *Descansos* is a bit like driving down a winding road; you won't know what's coming until you turn the page. Slow down and take in the scenery, maybe stop to admire the vista over a broken guardrail lit by candles and strewn with dying flowers. The beauty and the terror of the place, and the love and loss the offerings at your feet represent, are what this book is made of.

▲ ▲ ▲

About *RIFF*:

Creating *Descansos* was a challenge and an adventure. We threw the concept of the descanso out in a call for submissions, with no restrictions on style or genre, and we were happily surprised at the quality and variety of the responses we received. In fact, we enjoyed this adventure so much that we have decided to make it an annual tradition.

Descansos is the first in the Darkhouse Books new *RIFF* series. Darkhouse will throw out a broad concept to the writing world, and we will publish the best of what we receive, regardless of style or genre.

The concept of *RIFF* is to offer authors the freedom to create their own best pieces, free of common genre restrictions yet bound together by a common theme, the way jamming musicians build their own creations around a common melody. It sounds kind of crazy, but the book you are holding is evidence that it can work.

—*Susannah Carlson, Editor*
June 2017
Sunnyvale, California

*We begin our anthology with a series of vignettes that
are at once plainspoken and poetic, as we travel with the
author along dusty highways and forgotten byways.*

Shrine Stories

by Jesse Sensibar

I

Southwest Texas

He was 21.

II

Orange Grove, California

Found this one in the middle of thousands of acres of Cutie and Halo
orange and lemon groves on the edge of the Inland Empire on the
Old River Road.

III

Mexico Highway 1

Vandalized shrine to Samuel Mendez. Bus Driver. Highway 1 North
of Lorato.

IV

Stoneman Lake, Arizona

Arizona I-17 northbound at the 305-mile marker, at the start of a
sunset, when I can't hide my own shadow in the cross and my left

knee wants to collapse backwards underneath me. All I can do is kneel in front of this makeshift altar and bite my own tongue to keep from asking questions I'm afraid to answer.

V

Hermosillo, Mexico

Somewhere on the highway. These are the hardest parts. We could have died with you, but chose a different path.

VI

Old Kino Bay, Mexico

The Virgin changes a bit from place to place, context to context. Here she is on a wall in the Sonoran village of Old Kino Bay, a community that has existed and fed its people on the bounty of the eastern shore of the Sea of Cortez. We see the dolphins traveling parallel to the shoreline, mornings as we drink our tea and eat warm tortillas.

VII

Nogales, Mexico

More cartoon shrines to El Chilango down on the south side of the borderlands at the edge of the big truck economic zone. Takes so long for the commercial truck traffic to cross, it's no wonder the passing of time feels like death to Mexican transport drivers. Despite the wall and the heavy security, things still look much the same on both sides of the border town of Nogales. At the 21-kilometer edge of the zone, returning my temporary import permit, my nephew rode shotgun and I stopped to show him these shrines. We picked up a 300-peso statue of the Virgin of Guadalupe for a friend, worked our way back across the border, a few miles stretching to hours, then to Tucson, where, floating, we watched a falcon in the big mesquite beside the pool, until we made him nervous and he flew off with his dinner clutched in his talons.

VIII

Flagstaff, Arizona

A lazy highway patrolman and an inconsiderate person with a flat tire left me with an empty tow truck, empty pockets, and not much to do out here east of Flagstaff on Interstate 40 this Memorial Day afternoon, so I stopped by to visit you. You are a hard one to forget, Danny Boy. Hope you are smiling that sideways grin somewhere.

IX

Navajo County, Arizona

Headed home from the Cedar Fire, I found this roadside memorial to a lone Canadian northbound on Arizona Highway 77. It reminded me of one I stopped at for years until it completely disappeared, on Navajo Highway 15, just south of the community of Leupp, where a young Canadian couple died in a fiery head-on collision between their VW camper and a Ford pickup driven by a Navajo guy. Nobody survived. Days afterward, in the presence of an FBI agent who had been raised on the Pine Ridge Reservation and all four parents of the Canadian couple, in the towing yard, I used the winch on a tow truck to unfold the crumpled front end of the burned camper, in a vain attempt to locate and salvage their wedding rings, which they were known to keep stashed underneath the dashboard for safekeeping.

X

Highway 46

Backside of a memorial on Highway 46 near Lost Hills, east of I-5. The harvest seems to be tomatoes, garlic, and carrots right now.

XI

Daggett, California

Roadside shrine with a hand and a Bud Light sign, for a dog named Truck. Daggett is one of the roughest places I've ever been.

XII

Oracle, Arizona

Arizona Highway 77 Eastbound mile marker 93—David Chavez— "If love could have saved you, you would have lived forever."

Thebes—The Coming of War

by Terence Kuch

"Tearfully they bought keepsakes to send home… in the event of their deaths."
—Aeschylus, *Seven Against Thebes*

Here under the power lines
beside the ruined quag
is a shrine about as wide
as a mailbox; peaked roof, glass-
paned walls, a few drachmas,
candle on a flat dish,
a prayer copied out by hand.

Something must have happened here
by the road under the power lines,
here where trucks rush on to Athens.

Perhaps it has to do with
the drive-in over there
where men of Argos are drinking
wine, buying postcards, edging
spears, making plans
                              for Thebes.

The following memoir by Cate McGowan is a heartfelt, honest, and unflinching exploration of loss and love as she comes to terms with the death of her father.

I'll Go Now
by Cate McGowan

1.

THE other night, I tried to jumpstart an essay about Father's Day and how my dad died in a car crash. But the muse was bored with me, and my computer screen yawned as I stared and generated a single bland sentence. I needed to stress-eat. Salt and carbs. So, on the way to the grocery store to buy hotdog makings, the expensive kind I could only acquire across town, it dawned on me that I should make a pilgrimage to where my father drew his last breath. I'd sell the resulting essay to *The New Yorker* and become famous.

Earlier in the evening, a flash Florida squall had hit town at twilight. As I hit the road, the clouds still nudged thunder, and wet blacktop hissed under my tires. Lightning macraméd slipknots across the sky, and the highway was, as always, trafficky. It hadn't rained in Orlando in weeks, so the asphalt was greasy. I-4, which is always under heavy construction, twists through Orlando like a limber alligator, and the pavement's surface is uneven. If a driver doesn't have both hands on the wheel through the route's sharp meanders, well, it's easy to steer into trouble.

As I tooled along a particularly sketchy section of the road, nicknamed the Fairbanks Death Curve because many fatalities have occurred on those few yards of expressway, I glanced in my rearview mirror. Behind me, a rust Mercedes coupe was gaining on my bumper. No headlights on, it careened way too fast for conditions. The Merc's driver was NASCAR weaving. He swerved through lanes, zipped in front of me on two wheels at 65 miles per hour, almost clipped a pickup truck a car length ahead of me, and squeezed between us. Just then, the Merc skated out of control on the glassy surface and pirouetted in circles across three lanes. Time slowed and the car spun. And spun and spun.

All the brake lights of the autos around me flashed red in the puddles as we slowed to maneuver safely. Finally, the facsimile racecar, after a last spin, slid to a stop in the median, faced the wrong direction. I accelerated. But in my rearview, I could see the Mercedes' blinker. The car had righted itself and slunk to the side emergency lane, then disappeared as I got off at the next exit. I bought my chichi hotdog buns and designer wieners, though it took a few hours for my heart to slow. I had witnessed a near miss. No one had been hurt or even scratched a fender or a concrete pylon. A miracle? Who knows?

The coincidence rattled me. My father, many years ago, died in the same kind of accident, and I had just been trying to write about his last days and how, over the last two months, I'd been rear-ended three times while sitting at stoplights. I'd escaped those recent collisions unscathed. I have not escaped my father's accident, no matter how much I try to avoid thinking about it.

> *Three days before you died, I begged you to forget your business trip. We stood in the hall, and I stretched to my full height to kiss your face—one kiss for each day you'd be gone.* Here's one for Monday, one for Tuesday, one for Wednesday.

*I pecked your welted forehead and cheeks, swollen from the sap
of a poison ivy rash. The blisters seeped into your handkerchief
as you patted it against your swollen eyes. After your autopsy,
the coroner whispered to my mother that your lids were strangely
inflamed when he examined your body. Mom told me to never
mention your affected eyes, that we might be blamed for the
accident. All through my life, I've worried if my kisses made
your hives worse, spread the infection. And Dad, when you
were there in the silence before the ambulance arrived, I wonder
if the rain oozed and leaked into your broken car, the glass
shards no danger for a slumped corpse. Poison ivy is nothing
compared to ten tons of vehicle. If a seatbelt and a steel car
couldn't protect you, then I hope that rosary wrapped around
your fingers shielded your soul, provided solace as you passed
"instantly"—whatever that means.*

2.

I'm an orphan. My mother suffered like Jesus Christ until ten
years ago, when she drowned in her own fluids. And my father perished in a car accident when I was nine. Ever since Dad's passing, I've
whispered Yeats' poem "The Lake Isle of Innisfree" on repeat. Over
time, I've recited the poem out loud or in silence so often that I don't
even know I'm doing it, especially the last stanza:

> I will arise and go now, for always night and day
> I hear lake water lapping with low sounds by the shore;
> While I stand on the roadway, or on the pavements grey,
> I hear it in the deep heart's core.

And when I "go" there to Yeats' lines, I liken my repetitions
to saying the rosary or drumming impatient fingers to calm nerves. If
life gets me down, I mantra the words. Sometimes, I murmur the poem
when I'm about to slip into sleep or when I'm showering or brushing
my teeth. It's always comforted me. It's a prayer, a song.

It recently dawned on me why I obsessively repeat this
piece—I want to travel to the land of forgiveness. After my dad passed

away, I turned down the wrong road, and I've been looking for a U-turn ever since. Maybe if I could see where my father met his demise, touch the ground where he departed, create an anonymous descanso to honor him, everything would change.

> *Three weeks before you died, Dad, I had a nightmare. I threw off my sheets, ran into the kitchen, where you washed dishes with Mom. I was terrified of losing you, but you exclaimed,* Nobody's doing any dying around here! *I can't remember much else, but I bet you probably tweaked my nose or something else father-like. Maybe you smoothed my forehead. I do recall that you carried me back to bed. I believed you, trusted all was right. I wonder now: Three weeks later when you did die and go away for good, did you remember my prophecy when you were crushed on all sides?*

3.

My father was not lucky, and I've worried about his misfortune my whole life. He died young and unaccomplished, but loved by many. I've written poetry about it, tried to compensate with failed father-figure relationships and overachieving. How could someone live up to Dad's sainted status? His passing shaped me more than my Catholic upbringing or my deep disappointment at not being the daughter my mom wanted. I'm a neurotic, guilt-ridden woman who stays up late to check my grammar on social media. I keep most people at arm's length because I know they will leave me. And the people I do let into my heart ultimately break it.

Lately, I pass descansos and wonder at the flower bouquets, the decorated crosses, the dingy, weather-worn stuffed animals, seven-day candles still propped up in the grass, sometimes burning. Those *memento mori*, curated on medians and curbs, are places of active reverence. I wish I could do the same for my father. A gravestone is a cold, hard thing. When I visit a landscaped cemetery of the lined-up dead, it feels like I'm walking through a glorified file drawer. Graveyards are memorials in the land of the dead. Descansos are out here in the land of the living. We discover them in improvised, impermanent places. I find their random presence sometimes disturbing. I turn a corner, and, *bam*, I spy unexpected festival-colored fake flowers and teddy bears.

If only I could make my own descanso in the exact spot where my father died; to place my own poesy for Dad. I would leave a note for the others who died there, too. To what Alabama backroad would I travel? I'd journey there, but I have no clue how to find it. I can't locate obituaries in rural Alabama news microfiches and databases.

His accident went something like this. In a heavy thunderstorm, Dad drove down a two-lane state highway from Birmingham on his way home to Atlanta for my parents' anniversary. He hit a bad strip of road, and at 60 MPH, skidded sideways in the opposite direction. An 18-wheeler came up over the hill and slammed into him. Then a couple in a sedan like my father's came up the opposite hill and smashed into him, too, sandwiching his car. In the matter of a few seconds, three people were dead on the spot, and my father was wedged and trapped in the middle.

So how can I find where this happened? Sure, there's a police report sitting in the large secretary desk in my mom's home, but that place is now my sister's, and she and I haven't spoken in years.

When I was an adolescent (thirteen? fifteen?), I remember reading that police report. There were lots of lines of barely legible print that some Alabama state trooper scrawled across the form. It was scratchy and blasé sounding. Very matter-of-fact. It was a police report, not a sympathy card, after all. And the handwriting probably belonged to the same officer who called my mother the night Dad died. April 29.

Clipped to the multi-page document, was a photograph. I can see it clearly if I close my eyes. In the black and white coroner's picture, my father's big Chevy is a pinched, wobbly triangle the size of a small house. The vehicle was pummeled into an unrecognizable chunk of metal, like it had rolled down the side of a mountain a few thousand feet. In the picture, a man in uniform stands beside it and wears one of those Mountie-looking hats strapped to his chin. Lane markers move out of the shot on the wet highway behind. The driver's door is at least six feet off the ground—the officer's hat reaches the bottom of it. The door hangs slightly open. The front seat is ripped and stained.

There was no way to survive a crash like that.

4.

It was a late spring day in Atlanta. I remember it was warm enough that my mom rolled our dining room windows open halfway. We'd had dinner; it was after six, and I'd taken a bath. I was sitting in the living room, my legs draped over the arm of the sofa, reading a story for my third-grade English class. The tale was about the antics of a raccoon who stole macaroons. The rhyme was stupid, but I loved the idea of coconut cookies. The phone rang, and I looked into the kitchen as my mother picked up the receiver. Mom threw down the phone and ran up the driveway across the street and banged on the neighbor's door.

Now I know the trooper's words: "Ma'am, are you _____'s wife? Well, he died in a car accident today… No, I'm not kidding. Lady, I don't joke about things like that."

My mother would recount that conversation over and over as if our family's outrage about some man's insensitivity was something we could share and bond over. How could someone be so cruel to a new widow and her fatherless children? We hated that man all through my childhood. My mother's face would turn red every time she relived the moment she received the news. She never got out of the anger stage of grief. Now, I understand the man was probably tortured by having to deliver the facts of my father's accident; perhaps it was the most difficult phone call he ever made. Who were we to fault him or think he was an evil man?

Now that I don't really have any family to talk to, I want to go to where my father died, where he saw the sky and Earth for a last moment; go to where he had his last thoughts of love and fear. I would speak Yeats one last time: *While I stand on the roadway, or on the pavements grey*. Maybe I would only leave a pebble or a flower to mark the singular event that made me who I am in my "deep heart's core." Yes, I'll go. If only I can find the damn place.

> *Three weeks after you died, I lay in bed with my eyes tied open. I couldn't sleep. I was certain my nightmares, the ones you assured me would never come true but did, had augured your death and activated some terrible death path for you. It's so funny now, that I believed I had that kind of cosmic power. Yet my portent haunts me. You did die three weeks after I saw it in my dreams. And now, I don't remember you in detail; I can't recall your voice or your face, except what I see in photos. But I do recollect your hands and your broad fingers. The nails with white crescents, and clipped short, straight; your thick knuckles' black hairs sprouting in patches of freckle constellations. I took such care to notice those hands on the big man who never let someone talk him out of anything. Those hands, how they wrapped around your steering wheel when you took me to school that last morning.*

Thirteen

by Armine Mortimer

THIS is going to be a story about a boy who accidentally kills his mother. It will happen on his first birthday as a teenager. Since he was born on the thirteenth day of the seventh month, he always thinks of the number thirteen as lucky instead of unlucky, but on July 13, on the day he will kill his mother, the number thirteen will become unlucky for that day and for all future thirteenths and, strangely enough, for the thirteenths of the past too.

What will happen is this: his father will give him a hunting bow for his birthday, and the first time he tries it out, he will shoot an arrow into his mother. The arrow will penetrate her groin. She will not die from the wound, which will not damage any vital organs, as the arrow will narrowly miss both her uterus and her left kidney. Doctors will pronounce her lucky and send her home. But three days later, in spite of antibiotics and the lack of complications, she will suddenly die from what looks like a rapid and violent infection. Yet the autopsy will not explain the cause of death.

In this story, only the boy will know, deep down, what the pathologist cannot explain. It will be up to the story to uncover his secret.

What does a twelve-year-old soon to be thirteen know that his father doesn't? He will know what his father once may have known and will have forgotten: that he loves his mother and will never possess her. He loves his father too and does not blame him for possessing his mother. They go hunting together, but the boy does not have a weapon. His father shoots a deer with his bow, they follow it through the forest and find it slowly dying, it is a doe. The father tells the boy there may be a fawn not far off, and the boy understands it is up to him to find it, which he does. The fawn looks at him from deep within its velvety eyes, and the boy feels as if its eyes are shooting arrows, which inexplicably reach him even though he is unarmed. He will leave the fawn to its fate, and from that day he yearns to have his own hunting bow. But he will not know why until his thirteenth birthday. The boy knows only why his father shot the mother deer, and that he too will need a bow.

The story will have to reach July 13th before it can comprehend what will be going on in the boy's mind.

He will take up the bow and lay it tenderly across his lap, and he will stroke it from end to end. His eyes will follow his hand. Then he will realize his mother is watching him, and he will flush with pleasure. He will ask his father to take him hunting right away, to try out the bow and the arrows in their leather case. For the first time, he will feel himself a man, because he has a hunting bow like his father.

Later that afternoon they will go on a pretend hunt in the scruffy woods behind the house. It is not deer season. What will they shoot at? The story will look for an answer, but it will imagine what will be going on in the boy's mind the first time he chooses an arrow from the quiver, notches it, and pulls. He will be seeing in his mind's eye the imaginary doe beyond the point of his arrow, floating in the underbrush and quivering like the arrow. He will try to steady his stance, try to hold the doe still in his mind's eye, try to fix it in one spot, and yet her image floats. He is eager to let off his first arrow.

The father will quietly offer advice. He will choose a white flowering bush for a target. "Don't aim at it, pick a spot in front of it, on the ground. Hold it steady."

"Where?"

"I'll show you."

The boy will lower the bow. The father will stride ahead to the bush, counting his paces—twenty paces. He will turn and head back toward the boy—three paces. "Here. See this rock just ahead of me? Aim behind it two feet, right where I'm standing."

Will the temptation be strong, too strong? What will make the boy pull and release the arrow just then? Can't he wait till his father returns to his side? Will velvety eyes be looking at him from somewhere near the white bush? The story will seek answers to all questions.

In any case, the boy's first arrow will not fly where his glance wills it. A short, sudden cry, to the right of the bush, and father and son will run to the mother, pierced in the groin. The boy will faint. In the next days, he will be agitated.

The story knows, but it cannot tell, what anguish impels the mother to her death. When she dies, the boy will take his hunting bow into the woods behind the house and break it in two. He will leave the pieces in front of the white flowering bush.

*Our next story, by Tyson West, deftly threads the needle
between the real and the magical.*

Foota Forever
by Tyson West

"YOU ain't a real landlord until you've had a murder in one of your
units," the wiry gray haired man in jeans and an AC/DC sweatshirt
stated flatly, taking a sip of coffee.

Conrad, sitting across the booth, perked up and took a bite of
his pancakes.

"Ed, I've had skips, trash outs, drug busts, and bedbugs the
same as you, but I've never had a murder."

"Well, kid, just hang in there. Sooner or later you'll get one. It's
the nature of the business."

"Wait a minute, I've got that duplex on West Gordon, where
people keep leaving stuff in the alley. Some gangbanger got offed there
a month before I bought it."

"What do they leave?"

"Cheap jewelry with crosses, running shoes, open cans of

Steel Reserve 211, and Mexican candles in the tall glass jars with pictures of Our Lady of Guadalupe or Jesus on them. It is like a little shrine by the garage. They spray graffiti on the garage door, the number '13' and 'Santa Muerta'."

"You must have got a good price on the building."

"Oh yeah! The neighbors told me the kid got shot and accidentally killed by some other wannabe gangsta."

"Accidentally killed?"

"The cops told me most of the kids want to get wounded for street cred. Sometimes they push their luck just a little too far. The crime hasn't really hurt my renting the unit. Still, people would forget a lot quicker if it weren't for that damn shrine."

"Is it a pickup load or can you get rid of it in a garbage can?"

"It started out as a couple of those candles and a cross made out of shoes on the ground."

"What kind of shoes?"

"You know, athletic shoes… running shoes, basketball shoes. And there was a sign left that said, 'Love ya forever, Foota.' You've had murders. Has anyone ever left a shrine that won't go away?"

"I'm talking about murders in the unit themselves. I had that crazy guy that picked up the girl at the bus depot. He went off his meds and carved her up pretty good. We were cleaning blood from behind the radiator, and the carpet was a total loss. As soon as the cops let us take it out we rolled it up and tossed it. Funny thing, the way he got caught was he went into the emergency room to get meds, and he told them that he thought he might have killed someone. Then I had a heroin dealer blown away in my house on Eighth. But no one set up a memorial for either of them."

"I guess I'm not a real landlord because mine took place in the alley before I bought the place."

"You're showing promise. Hang in there, you'll get one sooner or later. When you've been in this business for thirty years, you will have seen just about everything."

Ed stood up and stretched, "Well Conrad, I've got to go meet the crew to clean up that estate house I just bought. It's full of cockroaches. The old guy was a hoarder. I hope we don't have to take it all the way back to the studs."

The two split the tab at the cash register, and Conrad got into his pickup to clean out a house from which the tenants had skipped in the middle of the night. On the way, he pulled through the alley by the duplex where Foota was shot, to see if the mess had grown back.

"Damn it, there's the cross of shoes again, and the candles." This time there was also a red satin heart from the dollar store. He parked his truck and was going to throw everything in the back to take to the dump with the garbage from the house, when a young woman strode up to him. Her hair was slicked back into a ponytail. She wore skintight jeans, and a snug, sleeveless tee-shirt that had written on it "Viva la Raza," and black wedge shoes.

He noticed immediately the tattoo on her forearm, "Te Quiro Foota," with a pair of red and blue running shoes crossed beneath the inscription.

"Do you think you could leave it here for a few more days? We're still trying to work through our grief."

Conrad was surprised at how softly she spoke in spite of how hard she appeared. "The City is on my back."

"Isn't it a public right of way?"

"Some of it is on the right of way all right, but a lot is on my property. Either way it's my responsibility to keep it clean. I got a letter from the City a month ago, and cleaned it up. The code enforcement officer said that I was fine. I told him it keeps coming back."

"Can't you just wait until you get another letter from the litter cop?" She asked with a gentle smile. Conrad noticed her rounded nose, like that of a Mayan Indian. She seemed sweet. Conrad had, however, learned not to buy into teenaged smiles, especially if it was a matter of rent. Since his duplex was fully rented and no one was complaining, he really didn't care about a descanso in the alley, so long as Code Enforcement left him alone.

"Okay. But the minute I get a letter from Code Enforcement,

I will toss it."

She smiled with her eyes this time, "Gracias. But I don't think you will get a letter from them for a while." Suddenly, her smile fell and her countenance hardened. "Besides, they say that if you disturb a descanso, you disrespect the dead. It will bring you bad luck."

"Oh, that's just a bunch of superstition."

"Do you see that doll?"

Conrad noticed a doll about a foot tall, a skeleton in robes. He felt a chill. He laughed in the tone of one whistling in the dark. "A Halloween decoration!"

"No, Señor, this shrine is under the protection of Santa Muerte."

Conrad nodded his head. "Yes, I see that." He had no idea what that meant but didn't want her to think he didn't know. "By the way, what's your name?"

"Maria Malverde."

"Did you know Foota?"

"You could say that."

He glanced down at the tattoo on her arm. "Is that a fresh tattoo or an old one?"

"You can say Foota is my once and future love. Like all great tattoos, it's a work in progress."

"Okay, I'll leave this stuff for now. But the minute the litter cop threatens me to clean it up, it's gone." She had dark, brown eyes that seemed as bottomless as the wells in the Yucatan Conrad had seen once in National Geographic. The black waters had swallowed human sacrifices.

"Gracias," she smiled sweetly again. As she turned away, her long, strong thighs rippled under her tight jeans.

He drove to his rental house five blocks away, backed up his pickup, and planned the loads to clean it out.

His helper, Jose, a wiry man in his thirties, arrived in his twenty-year-old Chevy pickup a few minutes later. The two of them began packing garbage bags and loading out furniture to Conrad's pickup, which had a high canopy on the back.

"Say, Jose, eventually we're going to have to clean up that mess behind the duplex on Gordon."

"What mess?"

"That shrine back there with those candles and shoes and statutes and half-empty cans of malt liquor."

"What kind of statues?"

"A skeleton in robes they call Santa Muerte."

"I'm sorry boss, but that's one thing that I will not touch. If Santa Muerte is protecting the shrine, it's dangerous to disturb it."

"What do you mean?"

"There was this Vietnam vet down on the corner of Mallon and Lindeke. He had that blue house on the corner."

"You mean the one with the chain link fence and the two-story garage?"

"Yeah. One of the Thirteens got killed back there. They put up descansos and a statue of Santa Muerte. Me and several other homeys warned that vet, but he was a really angry dude. He threw it all away, including the statue of Santa Muerte. He died of a fall off a ladder a week later. There's no way I'll touch that shrine. And you shouldn't either."

"How am I going to clean it up?"

"I don't know. Hire someone who doesn't know what he's doing. But everybody around here knows exactly what can happen."

Conrad wasn't superstitious, but he couldn't stop thinking of Santa Muerte or Maria Malverde as they mucked out the house and prepped it for painting.

▲ ▲ ▲

Three weeks later, a letter sent certified and first class from Code Enforcement arrived to announce that he had to clean up scattered garbage behind his duplex on West Gordon. Conrad winced.

He called Ed.

"Do you got anybody that you think can help me clean up?"

"Clean up what? You got your own boys."

"Well I got a place here that none of my boys will touch."

"Bedbugs or fleas or meth lab?"

"No. It's that shrine. Shoes, and candles, and stuff like that behind the house on West Gordon. You got anybody able to clean it?"

"No. If it's got a skeleton statue, they won't touch it."

"Well, the winos working for me know enough not to mess with La Flaquita or gangstas.

"To them it's more a matter of disrespecting them."

As he hung up, Conrad decided to see how far the City would push him.

Sure enough, two weeks after his deadline, he received another certified letter, this time from the city attorney. It threatened that they would condemn the property as a public nuisance if it was not cleaned up.

Conrad groaned. Maybe he could hire a professional cleaning service.

Eight calls later, he couldn't find anyone who would touch it.

"I guess I'll have to do it myself," Conrad groaned.

That Saturday night, an hour before sunset, he drove his pickup to the alley with a couple of garbage bags. He pulled in to load the shoes, candles, and malt liquor cans. He hoped if he left the statute of La Flaquita to continue to reign over the space, he might be spared the consequences of the curse, and the litter cop would not be likely to notice just one thing left.

No sooner had he gotten out of the truck than he heard a man's voice across the alley. "Hey, Mister Landlord."

Conrad turned and looked into the dark, brown eyes of a stocky, muscular young Mexican man. "I wouldn't touch that if I was you."

Conrad drew up tall and lowered his voice, "Well, the City says I got to do it."

The young man strode out of the shadows and faced Conrad. He was wearing baggy shorts just below his knees, a hoodie, expensive basketball shoes, and a San Diego Padres' ball cap backward over the bandana on his head. Conrad counted the gang tattoos on his calves, hands, and neck. He could also trace the outline of a large semi-automatic pistol in the pocket of his pants.

"I don't care what the City says. You do not touch La Flaquita or any part of any descanso protected by her."

Conrad often carried a gun, but he hadn't put it on that day. He had figured bullets wouldn't do much against a statue of bones.

"Okay, I'll just bear the consequences."

"Remember," the young man stood up straight. "La Flaquita is the queen of the dead. You don't want to join her before your time."

"Oh, no. I'll just let it be and let the City deal with it."

The dark man suddenly scowled, "I don't believe you. You're just going to wait until I'm gone. We're going to put somebody on this to watch it constantly. Since the shooting, I've never forgotten Foota. If you're not here any longer, no one else has the incentive to touch the shrine."

"I am truly sorry. I just said I would leave it alone."

The young man reached into his pocket, pulled out a black Glock, and pointed it at Conrad's heart. They both stood motionless and silent for what seemed an eternity.

A woman's voice cried from the shadows, "Hola, hombres!"

Conrad spoke up as she came from the darkness, "Maria, I'm so glad to see you."

The young man looked pale.

"Put down the gun, Fernando," she said firmly.

"Whatever you say."

"I don't want you to kill this man over what the City's making him do."

"But it's not me. I'm acting on behalf of Santa Muerte."

"No matter who put Santa Muerte's protection here, I can release it. You pick her up and take her with you. I want you to set this shrine up at your abuela's house, in the bedroom upstairs where we made love for the first time. You pray to her and to me in memory of me. Help him load up the bags, take everything and set it up there. It's time we left this alley."

She faded back into the shadows. It took all of Conrad's will to appear calm.

Fernando was shaking, "When Foota speaks, you don't question it."

Once the two of them had loaded the shoes and everything that they could into the garbage bags, Fernando gently picked up the statute of Santa Muerte. He rode with it in his lap to his grandmother's house. There, Fernando held the statue while Conrad carefully unloaded the bags and set them by the door to the house.

"You're lucky," Fernando said. "She likes you."

"I give her respect," Conrad whispered turning to leave.

"That is all she asks," Fernando replied.

Conrad turned to the skeleton. "When the time comes to face you, no matter if we call you Persephone, Hela, Mary, or Santa Muerte, that is all we'll have left to give."

Monuments of Absence
by Richard King Perkins II

Four bees just attacked me in my car.
I couldn't figure out where they came from at first,
but then I remembered the flower arrangement
I'd taken from the roadside memorial earlier this morning.
I'd intended on sorting them into a vase
before my wife got home, and giving her a thoughtful present.
That's just the kind of guy I am,
in case you were wondering.

Now I'm going to have to dump these white and red roses
on a back road somewhere and for good measure
I'm going to get rid of the garage sale signs
uprooted from at least a dozen different street corners
and the stack of flyers I took from the house for sale
a few blocks over.

No one is going to name a street or a park after me
when I'm dead,
so I'm creating monuments of absence instead,
placing little memories of things gone missing
into the minds of people I'll never know or meet.
It's not much of a legacy,
but I'm quite certain no one's naming a bridge or a school.
in your honor either.

Terresa Cooper Haskew is the author of our next story, a piece that uses thematic repetition to weave its eerie spell.

Living the Dream
by Terresa Cooper Haskew

I DIDN'T think so much about it when I pedaled home after work in the inky, achy darkness and found my bicycle had gotten there ahead of me. My metallic-blue ten-speed was leaning at the bottom of the stoop. Someone was playing mind games with me. Maybe my little brother, Carl.

He'd made off with my bike before, as a joke. That middle school mentality! But if that was true, what was this thing I had taken off on? This bike sure looked like mine, the one Dad gave me on my thirteenth birthday. Same size and color, same scratches. Okay, now that I was taking a closer look I could see that the seat was wrong. Maybe less worn and torn. Fewer memories? And fewer scrapes on the fenders. Well, someone was gonna be pissed.

Now I'd have to bring it back, back to whoever owned it when I wrenched it off the broken fence in front of Greenwald's Grocery.

My mother didn't like me to work the closing shift anyway, a girl riding home alone late, in the dark. But the money from Greenwald's was critical; Dad's life insurance barely kept a roof over our heads. He used to tell me, "Rachel, if you can dream it, you can live it." Well, that hadn't worked for him, because I knew we were his dream. But I bought into it anyway, bought myself a prom dress of gossamer white silk, and earned my own spending money. I often rode home with a plastic sack swinging from my handlebars, full of Mr. G's generosity. Yeah, Mom would be tonight's second pissed person when I told her I had to get this bike back to the store, then turn around and study for the last of my finals.

Dropping the ride beside my own, I started up the steps to the stoop. The wrought iron rail was cold in my hand, and the way was dark. No one thought to leave on a light. I was only slightly out of breath from the pedaling, but I suddenly seemed to have little energy. The steps were steep, sweating cement secreting a limestone scent, and those steps were as familiar as my own face. Yes, this freckled reflection was firmly fixed in my mind from all the mooning in the mirror over my gorgeous neighbor, Sam. I used to pile my auburn hair on top of my head and parade before the dresser, imagining myself gowned like an angel for prom, Sam waiting at the door with an armful of pink roses. He actually asked me last week!

I knew there couldn't be more than three, maybe four risers to reach the stoop. In the gloom, I could make out our address on the weathered siding, 127. I guess too many hours on Greenwald's gray linoleum had taken a toll, because the top of the stairs was just too far away. I had to sit on the slick steps to rest. Sore toes wiggled inside my dingy white Nikes, flexing to the cadence of crickets echoing in my ears.

▲ ▲ ▲

I didn't think so much about it when I pedaled home after work in the inky, achy darkness and found my bicycle had gotten there ahead of me. Seems I recalled this happening before, though the fatigue of 60-hour work weeks at the *Herald* was enough to dumb me down. It was the job I had always wanted. Funny thing. the *Herald* headquarters was located where Greenwald's store used to be, right on the corner of Beale and Spring. Though the newspaper's new building covered nearly the whole block, the old mangled fence still stood beneath a gnarled oak. The site held a pervasive odor of burning rubber and exhaust fumes. Someone had erected one of those annoying white crosses, draped with a shawl of faded pink flowers. It was still a good place to park a bike.

I had hurried home, pedaling fast despite the long day. Racing under the street lamps, my marquee-cut engagement ring caught the occasional ray, flashing tiny bursts like northern lights. I nearly hit the curb, staring star-struck at Sam's ring. When he said, "Let's do it, Rachel," he was my proof that dreams really do come true. If you want something bad enough, you can make it happen. Our wedding was a month away. When I slowed to a stop, I saw my bike, again already waiting at the front of my house. Wasn't Carl too old to play jokes on me?

The front door opened as I stomped down the kickstand of someone else's Schwinn. I looked up to the silhouette of my mother, backlit by the golden glow of our living room light. She hadn't aged a day, it seemed. I hoped to inherit her perpetuity.

"I lived through another night!" I called, waiting to hear her relief at my arrival, wanting to hear her familiar voice. The outline of her tilted head said she was listening, but wasn't sure what she'd heard. I called again as I started up the steps, but the door closed.

▲ ▲ ▲

I didn't think so much about it when I pedaled home in the inky, achy, darkness and found my bicycle had gotten there ahead of me. Seems I was always slow these days, slow enough for the bike to beat me home. I couldn't quite remember where I'd been, but the seat beneath me felt familiar and the destination right. Drifted leaves crackled under my wheels. The pedals arced over and over beneath my feet, an automaton hurling me homeward. My hips hurt at the peak of each rotation, a geriatric groan of bones. Chill wind blew a strand of hair across my mouth; I glanced down to hook it out, was dismayed to find it not grayed, auburn still shone in the artificial light. With ribs heaving, I coughed up something copper, knew there was no time to rest. Sam would be waiting for his medicine, for his sip of water from the yellow Tupperware tumbler, for me to button up his plaid pajamas, pull the comforting quilt over his sunken chest, just the way he liked it.

I laid the borrowed bike at the foot of the steps, and paused to study my own ten-speed. Blue paint was eroded and stained the color of rust. My handlebars were twisted, the front tire bent forever out of round. I touched the black rubber handle, and fear rose in my throat at the sight of my hands. My fingers lay smooth and slim across the grips, without the warp of age. There was no display of veins on the backs of my hands, which I had imagined hovering over Sam's furrowed brow. Looking down at my shoes, those same worn Nikes, I realized they were caked with something like mud, or was it dried blood?

With my foot on the first step, I heard a distant voice, low and familiar. Just down the sidewalk, beyond the pool of poor sodium light, a man stood, tall and straight. Though I could not see his face, I knew him immediately. He told me the dream was done; it was time to come home.

Our next story, by D. Dina Friedman, is at once dreamlike and heartbreaking, as the author explores the border between the unlimited expanse of a child's imagination and human helplessness in the face of the inevitable.

Flying
by D. Dina Friedman

Her father taught her the laws of physics. Spread your arms like propellers, one palm facing the wind, the other facing away. In the yard, she spins and spins, never losing patience. It may take a couple of hours before she's going fast enough to take off, she says. Will I watch?

Her mother has just called and told me that the X-ray has revealed a spot on her father's lungs, the father who taught her the principles of physics. All she's doing is following the principles of physics. Why can't her arms work the same way as propellers? She starts to wobble, fall toward the ground, but my son takes her hand and they spin together. Sooner or later, he's sure they'll take off. They are seven years old, and he wants to marry her. He introduces her to all the neighbors as the girl he's in love with.

It's a principle like the principles of physics that spots on the lung don't recede easily. No guarantee that a miracle drug will do the trick, or a good attitude, or relentless spinning. I make the mistake of telling them they can't really fly because I want to go inside and wipe counters, or dust, or do a hundred other things to order my life against spots. She stares at me with her chocolate cookie eyes. "You're wrong. I can fly," she says, as a hawk circles the mountain behind us, soaring over the newly turned foliage. Then she asks for a ladder so she can climb onto the roof and take off.

"Sorry. No flying while I'm responsible for you!" I close the door, making a pretense of folding clothes as I watch them out the window attaching a kite to a wagon. She sits inside hopefully, preparing for liftoff, as my son vroom-vrooms her down the hill. When the wheels stay on the ground, he vroom-vrooms louder. They try again. And again. They keep trying until it's time to drive her home. There's a babysitter at the house. Her mom's with her dad at the hospital, watching him lean into pillows, breathing suddenly as difficult as flying.

The next day my son comes home from school and tells me all about the invader zombies engulfing her father's body. He's going to help her fight them. She's going to fly to his house, and then he'll fly with her to the hospital. He goes outside to wait for her, spinning until the ground falters beneath him. In the sky, hawks circle, occasionally divebombing for mice. In the hospital, her father dreams about physics. Her mother said he blew out this disease years ago, when chances of survival were rare. A miracle. And now?

I press an iron against the sheets. When they are stacked, I go outside, where my son is still spinning himself into furious falls. His back against the grass, he suddenly points at the sky. There. Coming out of the clouds. A girl with wings.

The Road to Paihia
by Frank Russo

The car behind tail-gates as we twist round corners
stuck between second and third gears.
We don't dare pass the Kombi on these bends.
Ferns anchored to cliff faces, the roadside strewn
with crosses, white splints nailed together.

> ...*for the safety of people visiting accident sites in potentially*
> *hazardous locations,*
> *crosses should not be encouraged as memorials*

The jagged silhouette of Bream Head rises above the sea,
a skinny kid in board shorts dives in. A single
white cross pinned to a telegraph pole, marking
where a car left the road.
Behind us, the man in the Subaru
overtakes, accelerating into the curve,
placing his trust in fortune.

> *Crosses should be constructed of tantalised timber*
> *with a cross section not exceeding*
> *75mm x 50mm ... painted white ... to a standard that will maintain*
> *colour and appearance when exposed to the weather for a minimum of five years.*

On a granite outcrop, someone has stenciled in white paint:

MAMU
JESUS
DIED
FOR
YOU

The ring of forest is thick with beech and matai.
A billboard on the roadside says 'Tell him if he's speeding,'
a woman's eyes flashing wide and yellow.

> *Crosses should not be erected where remedial works*
> *have been undertaken ... or if the character of the road*
> *has been altered ... [to] change the circumstances that led to the accident.*

Angling through a hairpin,
we face another set of three—
a miniature Golgotha marks the spot
where a family left this earth,
winding their way on the road to Paihia.

Amber Colleen Hart presents us with a piece that beguiles
with normalcy while offering the reader an unflinching look at
life after a partner's death.

After Your Husband Dies – An Instruction Manual
by Amber Colleen Hart

Week One

Aᴛᴛᴇᴍᴘᴛ to start the riding lawn mower. Turn the key several times and listen to the engine stutter. Assume you've flooded the carb. Get out the push mower. Curse the design of the ripcord. Stomp the mower base, kick the wheels, try again. Mow the perimeter. Move in closer until practically turning circles in the center of the yard. Four hours thirty-seven minutes later, remember what he said every time he got done mowing in the heat, "It's Africa-hot out there."

Vacuum the living room, back and forth, back and forth. Wait as long as possible before disturbing the pattern to walk into the kitchen. Brew the usual amount of coffee. Use his NY YANKEES mug. Take the handle in your left hand like he did and place your mouth where his mouth rested every morning. Note how the coffee tastes bitter. Dump the remainder down the sink, wash the carafe, measure out half the amount of grounds for tomorrow.

Week Two

Get off the phone with longtime friend who keeps saying *time heals all wounds*. Congratulate yourself for quelling the urge to tell her to shove her uninvited sentiment up her non-widowed ass. Opt instead to do the next thing. Consult the calendar. Drive to the drycleaner without a seatbelt.

Answer the pimply faced boy behind the counter who's asked in a half-sentence, "Picking up?" and "Last name?" Blank out when he begins an explanation about there being a stubborn stain on one of the button-down Oxfords. Tune back in at the end of the sentence.

"...try again, but it probably won't make a difference."

Let the boy behind the counter wait. Contemplate how he would react to learning the owner of the shirt now rests in a "modestly priced" urn buried in the back of a closet. Ashes to ashes. Rub at the indentation the weight of the hangers has left in the crook between forefinger and thumb. Drive home without remembering which route you took.

Hang the clothes next to where his one-and-only suit used to rest before adorning his body one last time. Dust to dust.

Week Three

Sleep on and off, minutes at a stretch. Turn on the fan, turn off the fan. Let the dog on the bed, kick the dog off the bed. Watch a black-and-white movie with actors whose names you never knew and a plot you can't discern. Wake up with a familiar headache, like a hangover from days long gone. During the day, fall asleep sitting up and ruin the chances of a good night's rest. Vacuum a new pattern into the carpet. Make half a pot of coffee. Pour a cup in the fine china that hasn't been used since his mother's wake. Set the cup on its matching saucer, careful not to make a noise.

Stare out the kitchen window at a robin plucking a worm from the rain-moistened ground.

Week Four

Doze on the couch. Allow death to creep in and place a memory before you like a cat dropping a dead mouse at your feet. Remember Kyle Miller on the grass next to his pool—blue lips, eyes in a fixed gaze. His father scanning the partygoers' faces for answers. As if one of the nine-year-olds in the crowd was responsible for Kyle diving in head first just like he, Mr. Miller, had warned all of you not to. See yourself cowering behind friends, stuffing a second cupcake into your mouth, wondering why it suddenly tastes so bad.

Swallow down the variances of grief. Forgive yourself for not realizing that one death does not weigh the same as another.

Week Five

Gaze out the kitchen window. Do not blink at the robin that's come back to poke at the spent leaves for another worm. Observe a bee hovering over a wilted zinnia blossom, unaware the next morning's dew will kill the flower. Accept that everything dies. And everyone. Wonder what the point had been to love him like you did.

Resent him for patting your hand just before he died, and asking your name again. Turn from the window. Pitch his NY Yankees mug into the box marked "Goodwill."

Week Six

Fill your calendar with tasks to keep him from monopolizing the day. Ignore his musky scent of Old Spice and Marlboros, forget his gap-toothed smile showing off the dimple in his cheek. Give up. Sink down into his tobacco-laden breath. Feel his hair tickle your neck, the squeeze of his arms around you.

Panic when the warmth of his presence dissipates into the image of his vacant stare—just like Kyle's. Mr. Miller is staring at you again, like everything is your fault.

Run to the kitchen. Retrieve the NY Yankees mug from the box. Cradle it against your chest.

Week Seven

Note that the robin is outside again, pecking another worm, stretching it free from the earth. Pound on the window and yell, "Shoo.

Go! Leave it alone!" Stare down the robin as it cocks its head then uproots another worm.

Dash outside under the maple tree. Curse the fleeing bird. Ignore the rainwater dropping from the leaves onto your head as if warning. Stop. Stop. Stop. Hitch up your sodden socks. Trudge back inside, careful not to glance at the neighbor's house.

Stand in the shower until all the hot water runs out.

Week Eight

Return to the drycleaners with his stained button-down Oxford. Greet the boy behind the counter with a curt hello. Explain, with some restraint, how the stain on your husband's shirt needs to be removed. Explain, with less restraint, that your husband is dead.

Add, "Cremated, by the way. Burnt to a crisp."

Allow the boy to stumble over his words. Resent the fact he's called you "Ma'am."

Forget how to inhale, exhale, or even move your mouth. Try to staunch the onset of tears that don't really feel like grief. When the boy cocks his head in confusion, much like the robin, cock your head back at him. Decide which of you is the robin and which the worm. Wait while the little fucker wriggles about in search of an answer to the question you haven't asked.

Utter the word, "Tomorrow," in a threatening tone.

Vow to never go back there again.

Week Nine

Mow the lawn.
Straight lines back and forth.
Back and forth.

*Our next story, by Brian Morgan, is an exploration of
self-acceptance in the face of grief.*

A Song for the King

By Brian Morgan

I REMEMBER *looking at the cast album liner of the original Broadway production
of Joseph and the Amazing Technicolor Dreamcoat when I was thirteen years old.
I remember not recognizing a single name. When I met Tim Fauvell years later,
he mentioned he was on the album. I looked again. I had known his voice since I
was a kid.*

▲ ▲ ▲

I remember moving to New York five years later to attend
theatre school, and that's where I met you. You were young, half-black,
white teeth, muscular. You brought a fish tank to our dorm room,
which was really just a seedy hotel on 86th street, a one-bedroom
apartment that slept three people, when one of us didn't have a friend
over, which was never. You bought two Oscar sharks, both babies,
from a place on 79th Street. We called them Flip and Flipper because
they smacked their tails against the top of the water. We thought Flip

ate Flipper because one morning there was just one fish, but we later learned that Flipper got caught up in the air filter system, behind the black, where nobody could see him, dead there for weeks before he was found.

Flip once jumped out of the tank, and I thought we couldn't do anything, let him die, his mouth agape, his skin like spikes to us. We couldn't pick him up. I was willing to let him go, but you picked up a piece of paper, looked at me like I was terrible, slipped it under his body, and put him back in the tank, where he continued to swim. You were kind to never mention that I was willing to let him die.

▲ ▲ ▲

I remember when I graduated school, you had already left. You were with the *Jesus Christ Superstar* tour then, with Ted Neely. You replaced Dennis DeYoung, formerly of the rock band Styx, who played Pontius Pilate before you did. You said he showed you his chord progressions for *Don't Let Me Stop Your Great Self Destruction*. It upped it a third. But you can sing it, I said. You said you were in New York, playing at the Beacon. Did Karen and I want to go for a beer? No, I said, we were tired.

I remember thinking I wasn't that tired. You found your love, you said to me, about Karen. Yeah, it's going well, I said. I wasn't tired. I said No because I worked a temp job and you were on tour with Ted Neely. I said No because it took me eight years of voice lessons to sound like you sounded when you were eighteen years old. I didn't write you. I didn't call. When you were cast in the original production of *Lion King* I vowed never to see it. I was in summer theatre making $175 a week, doing another mediocre version of *Oklahoma*.

I was glad when you weren't nominated for a Tony award. Karen and I watched the Tonys together that year. I wanted *Lion King* to lose to *Ragtime* and I was angry when *Lion King* won. Rosie O'Donnell, who hosted, mentioned you by name. They sang the *Circle of Life* for the television cameras, and I remember how happy I was that I didn't have to watch you from my 300-square-foot studio apartment in Jersey City, with mousetraps. You weren't in that number. Karen wanted to fuck and I refused her, not because I had a girlfriend, although I did, but because intimacy is so opposed to self-pity that to perform, I would have had to let up the anger. It would have been too much.

▲ ▲ ▲

I remember, when we met, you didn't have anyone. Your parents shipped you off to boarding school for high school. You never went to college. Your mother sent you a rain stick for your birthday one year. It shook in the package. Another fucking rain stick, you said, as if she had always sent you one. She's fucking weird, you said. You embraced me when my parents got divorced and when I screamed at my mother. You told me I was the only one at school who got you. You're smarter than I am, you said to me once, and more mature. I said I'd give it all away for your voice.

I remember that voice. That classically trained rock 'n' roll musical voice, a voice I had never heard before or since, except maybe a kid named Lambert who won *American Idol* a few years back. Ted Neely seems to do a retirement tour of *Superstar* every year. I saw, perhaps, his eighth. He was like seventy years old. The Pilate couldn't sing it. Dennis DeYoung would have laughed at the idea of the progressions for that guy. Like giving progressions to a frog. The show misses you. It misses your power, your innocence, your anger. Your sense of injustice.

I remember walking into the Virgin Megastore on Fourteenth Street, back when there were record stores, just after you recorded *Lion King*. There was a CD single behind a tab with your stage name on it, "Jason Raize, Simba in *Lion King*," it said on the album cover. I didn't pick it up. I rushed out of the store, lightheaded. Hating myself for hating you. And I did hate you. I hated you for being the most naturally gifted singer I've ever met, and for being kind to me.

I remember Rosie O'Donnell interviewed you and adored you. I met her years later when I worked with a band on her cruise ship for gay and lesbian families. You were dead by then. You had been dead a long time, maybe ten years. I wanted to mention you to her but I didn't. Not because I was afraid, for the first time, of how I would feel if somebody called you the most talented person they'd ever met; but because I wasn't sure what I would do if she didn't remember you at all.

I remember reading that you killed yourself in Australia, working as a farmhand, nearby a boy that you loved, a world-renowned glass sculptor. They didn't find you for three days after you hanged yourself. That still strikes me. I could name fifty people who knew you and loved you and for whom you were a constant barometer of failure—against the image of you, we fought for every voice lesson, every audition. Every time we stepped on a stage we were aware that we were not you, and yet, despite all of that energy in the world pushed toward you, you hanged yourself in the one place in the world where no one would look.

They didn't know who you were. A farmhand. They didn't know how you sounded. They didn't know the voice that was being choked out of that throat when you stepped off the stool. Three days you rotted. I've not gone three days without thinking about you since the day we met.

▲ ▲ ▲

Three days ago, twenty years after you recorded it, I listened to *Lion King* for the first time. I downloaded the MP3. It's not everything you were capable of, but there are moments. They wrote you a shit song made to look like a great song, but you did well with it. Your voice, that compelling mix of gospel and classical with David Bowie's guts, it's good, but they missed you: what made you great was that you picked up the fish with a piece of paper and then sang as if you were angry at everybody who gave up on it. Elton John didn't know that about you when he wrote the song for you.

For too many youthful years, all I wanted was for you to fail—it would have made me feel better about Elton John never writing a song for me; and all I want to do now is write Elton John a letter and ask him to write you a better song, so you can sing it posthumously. He saved the fish, I would tell him. He was a better friend to me than I was to him, I would say. He didn't know the pressure on that performance. That in the end, it would be the only thing left of you.

It is unfair to chastise Elton John for your suicide, but I admit being disappointed with what's left. For twenty years, I wanted no one to know who you were. And now I don't want anyone to forget.

When *Rent* was casting originally, you were touring.

They did it here last weekend, where I teach undergraduates in Brooklyn. A student of mine was in it. He is going to leave the college to pursue theatre. You went there? he asked, when I told him where we went to school and offered to help him. He mentioned Jesse Tyler Ferguson, Gretchen Mol. He mentioned your former understudy, Christopher Jackson. I didn't mention you. He wouldn't have known. He was probably five years old when you recorded *Lion King*. You're a name on an album liner.

They're moving on without us, Jason. *Lion King* is still running here. Disney still makes films, even though you haven't sung in one in fifteen years. They'll publish novels, regardless of whether or not I write them. It goes on. I searched on Amazon for your solo CD, and I found two singles I could purchase for a penny each. I didn't realize you never made a whole album. I'm sorry to hear that.

I remember thinking, when I heard you'd hanged yourself, that you wouldn't have done it if I had returned your calls or been nicer to you or been less jealous. I don't think that's true. I think you would have done it anyway, that it was long in your cards, that you needed so much more from life than there was to get, and I, certainly, was incapable of getting any more for you. But it's not an excuse. You made my life better, and I regret not trying to make your life better, not as much as I could have, not as much as you deserved. You deserved better from me, not because you recorded albums, but because you picked up the fish. I'm sorry I didn't pick up the fish.

I don't believe in heaven, not really. I don't believe you can hear this, read this, experience this. But I remember, Jason. It's the one last thing I can do for you. I remember.

*Our next story, by Ivan Faute, is as
quirky as it is surreal.*

Watermelon Baby

by Ivan Faute

MIKE took the baby and plunged it into the water. In three times. Out three times. He counted to five each time, his mouth forming the words, but he didn't make any sound. He decided on a count of five right after he had driven out of the hospital parking lot. "Five's a good number," he had said to Jane.

"It's not a very complete number," she'd answered him. She'd been fussing with the corners of the blanket that covered the child.

"But it's a good long time. Longer than you would think," he'd said. He kept reminding himself that the count was going to be five; real slow he'd count to five. He wasn't sure why he had to keep reminding himself, but he was aware that he wanted to. And now that he was actually putting the baby in the water, the count seemed too long, but also seemed something that had been decided already, so he couldn't make adjustments. The baby was more mottled and wrinkled than Mike had expected. It was also stronger; it squirmed in his fingers, twisting its head about, flexing its limbs at the wrist and the elbow and the shoulder, all at the same time, it seemed.

"You sure that's okay?" Jane asked. She stood over his shoulder, looking down into the sink. It was a deep, square sink molded out of concrete, with a simple pipe for a faucet and a rubber stopper.

Mike finished his count before he acknowledged her. By then it was all done anyway. "I decided on a five count," he said. "You are the one said we had to do it three times."

She took the child from him like it was a cat, like it might try to claw its way out of her arms and scratch her on the way down her leg. She examined it all and held it up to her face to listen to its breathing. She wrapped it back in its blanket then. "Three's the proper number," she said. "The Father, Son, and Holy Spirit."

"I know all that," Mike interrupted. He didn't want to get her started talking. "Let's keep on," he said. He looked out the door of the janitor's closet, but no one else was about. The highway rest stop was quiet so early in the morning, and while there were two-dozen cars in the parking lot, and just as many eighteen-wheelers, no one was using the toilets or buying anything from the vending machines. The couple walked to the car without talking. The pulsing rumble of the truck engines covered any noise of their footsteps.

Jane spoke over the roof of the car. "He's smaller than I thought he'd be."

"Of course," Mike said. "He's not even grown enough to be born yet."

Mike slid into the car quickly and tried to cover the dome light with his hand. He could make out the shadowy shape of his bones inside his fingers. Jane clenched her teeth, adjusting her bottom on the seat, which was as long and deep as a couch. "It hurts to set," she said.

"Shush," Mike told her. "Close the door quiet."

She pulled the door heavily until it clicked, with the baby cradled in one elbow. The baby shivered. "I'll turn the heat on high," Mike said.

"It's asking God for a prayer is all," Jane said.

Mike pulled away, but didn't turn on the headlights until he got to the highway. He had turned the dashboard lights low, but he checked the knob again. He couldn't keep his hands still and kept checking the heat and the lights and every knob. He looked behind him to see several pairs of white lights, but couldn't tell if they belonged to cars or trucks, or how far away they were. "It's so flat here. You can't tell how far apart things are even." He still spoke in a low voice.

"They won't know yet. Not till light," Jane said. She spoke at a regular pitch, louder than either of them had spoken since they'd left the hospital. Mike let the words hang there before them both. The words were like glass, hard, but clear and fragile.

He drove on, both hands on the steering wheel, looking in his mirror at the far-off lights trailing him, looking at Jane and the baby beside him. Jane sat low on the seat, her knees butting against the glove box, the baby laid out across her belly and pelvic bone. Mike couldn't tell if the child was asleep or not, but Jane kept fussing with the blanket and the thick flip of hair that seemed to be stuck to the baby's forehead like a bow.

"Are you warm enough?" he asked. "Is it warm enough?"

"All's fine," Jane said. She didn't look at him, but kept fussing.

It was quite a few miles down the road before they found an open gas station. Mike had started to worry that the car would peter out and he'd have to hike along, carrying the gas can that was in the trunk. He didn't want to leave Jane and the baby alone in the car; too many things could happen on a highway.

The station was old and a bell rang inside the building when he pulled beside the pump. The attendant was watching a small black-and-white television set on the counter and never looked at Mike's face. "How far's Marmaduke?" Mike asked.

"Why you want to go there?" the man said, still focused on his television.

"How far is it?"

"It's thirty miles or so. No reason to go there though, just watermelon fields and a cotton barn."

Mike took his three dollars in change. "Thank you."

Jane was singing in a low voice when he got back to the car.

"He says it's thirty miles on."

"I know how far it is," Jane answered.

"You've never even been there," Mike said.

"I know where it is anyway."

"Well anyway," Mike said, "that means Arkansas is just a few miles ahead."

"Just a few," Jane said. She looked over at him when she spoke. "I know what I'm doing. I know you don't think so, but I do."

A car pulled up to the other pump and the bell went off inside the station. Jane sank further down in the seat and Mike pulled out, fiddling with the radio knob. A few more minutes and they made the state line. "There's the sign," he said.

Jane smiled at him. She mouthed the words, "Welcome to Arkansas."

Mike looked for the mile signs, old yellow reflectors that counted down the miles. The sun started to come up on his left and illuminate the cotton plants. They had dark, glossy leaves stuck with yellow or red blossoms, in no order it seemed to him. Every few miles, there would be an open field that looked sort of empty and neglected, but Mike could see watermelon vines spread all among the random cotton plants or corn stalks that had grown wild. There were also six-foot-tall thistles and the long, feathery pokers of ragweed spread about. The farmers didn't spray those fields as much.

Jane sat up in the seat and put the baby flat on her thighs. "It's just," she said, "if we look at a weather map we are scientists, but if we look at the clouds, and understand them, we are superstitious."

"I'm not arguing with you," Mike said. "I got a car and got you out like you asked." They'd had the same conversation right after they left the hospital. Mike didn't understand her then either, but he trusted Jane. He felt like she had some sort of authority.

Mike looked over at her, down at the baby in her arms, then

out at the glossy green leaves boxing them in on either side. Jane spoke to the brightening sky. "They say I'm backwards, but I think it's seeing that the world, meaning time and such, isn't so much a long line as it is a big mess. A big jumble. Like a scribble on a napkin."

"I'm not arguing," Mike answered.

Thirty miles along, instead of a mile marker, there was a two-foot green sign with the name "Marmaduke." Mike pulled over and turned off the car. On their side of the road was a melon field and on the other side, a cotton patch. Mike went around to help Jane out. He took her hand and they walked into the midst of the plants. When they'd gone a few hundred feet, Jane knelt. She lifted her arms straight up, locking her elbows, holding the baby aloft.

"Down here," she yelled out. "It's here." Her words spread out thinly, covering the space, the vines and stray cotton and corn plants, the maples and cypress and pines that marked off the property line. Jane swiveled her head and breathed heavily. Mike walked behind her, back and forth, stepping over fruit and making impressions in the thin dust.

"How long?" Mike asked.

"Hush," Jane answered sharply. She held up the baby for a long time; its arms and legs whimming out and around. The sun spread out and touched them, so the car was no longer just a dark color, but clearly blue, and the wet film on the pavement dried off. Some blackbirds with red splotches on their shoulders circled above, then swooped down to get a better look. Jane's arms began to shake a little at the elbow. Mike noticed that her breathing was shallow and the muscles all up and down her arms quavered a bit. He thought about what would happen if she dropped the infant, and then, just like the thought made it happen, the baby tumbled out of her hands. Its fist, swaddled in fat and dimples, hit Jane on the forehead and left a pink circle. The child hit the dirt with a thud and Mike was afraid to look. Instead, he focused on Jane's hands, still flattened out and open to the sky.

"Look," Jane said. She had her face turned to the ground. "I told you," she said.

Mike looked down at the baby spread out at Jane's knees stuck in the dirt. The baby had split open. Not just its head, but its body too, right down the middle. The arms and legs had broken off as well. The shock of the red against the hard, brown dirt and the yellow sunshine hit Mike's eyes so forcefully, he was blind a moment. When his eyes adjusted to the sight, he saw that mixed in with the red were specks of black, and his eyes corrected some more, and he saw that the red was not blood at all, like he had known it would be, but, instead, the baby had been full of melon flesh and seeds.

"We can plant all these now," Jane said. She started to pick out the flat seeds, which might have been lacquered, they were so shiny and wet. "We can plant all of them and raise our own family."

The Best Revenge

by Ellaraine Lockie

*"On Thursday 7 July 2005 a series of four bomb attacks
struck London's public transport system… 56 people killed,
700 injured." —Wikipedia*

By my annual October trip to London
I have buried the exploded British bodies
under Katrina's casualties
But still can't take the bus two kilometers
from Euston Station to St. Margaret's Hotel

Suitcases too heavy to lift into a bus I tell myself
Losing my first private battle against terrorism
as I pull two suitcases and herd the third
down Upper Woburn Place
All the while awarding myself a walking ovation
for having flown the day after 9/11

Self importance goes worldwide at Tavistock Square
where a woman's professional camera
equipment blocks the sidewalk
And leaning against a park fence
is a garden-sized plastic bag spilling bouquets
and the budding bloom of a young girl's face
Her glossy paper smile gazing at the overcast sky

And I know instantly the sun hasn't smiled
on her parents since the seventh of July

I don't need to hear from the photojournalist
how Tornado Hussain lifted the roof
off a double-decker bus
How it twisted through the air
And set passengers down on nearby walls
in three-dimensional red globs
A movement from a school of terrorist abstract art

Later I stand in ambiguity
Body fixed by fear in front
of Russell Square's tube window
Mind correlating the risk of a one-time ticket
with an economical week's worth

Summoning courage to connect
with Brits passing me by
Who wear IRA history as casually as the scarves
relaxing around their necks
They buy their ways into the burial chamber below
Where another shrine waits
To remind us that retaliation can be as peaceful
as purchasing a public transit ticket

The following story, by Kurt Newton, is a classic horror tale with a creative twist.

Angels of Mercy, Angels of Grief
by Kurt Newton

Tʜᴇ teenaged girl stood along the roadside, her car idling on the shoulder, a small bouquet of yellow daffodils in her hand. The ground at her feet was gouged, the marks formed by a straight-line pair of tire tracks that ended abruptly at the foot of a large tree. The tree stood defiant, only a small patch of bark torn from its trunk. A clot of flowers and plastic hearts and handmade signs covered the ground beneath the wound. "WE LOVE YOU, JULIE." "WE MISS YOU, JULIE."

"Excuse me."

The girl jumped. She turned and took a nervous step back into the grass as the stranger approached. There were tears in her eyes.

"Huh?"

"You knew her, didn't you?" the man asked.

"Uh, yeah... from school. Julie was my friend."

"Are these all from her friends and her family?"

"You mean the flowers?"

"Everything."

"I guess so."

"What about that one?" The man pointed to a circular object attached to one of the tree's exposed roots. It looked like a pretzel made of wood. "The cross. Did you see who left that one?"

The girl looked. She didn't see what the man was pointing to. "I don't know. It could have been anyone. Are you from Julie's family?" Her eyes searched the man's face.

"I'm sorry to bother you," he said, and walked back to his car. The girl watched him leave.

The man took one last look at the memorial beneath the tree. Something seemed to glow between the flowers. He tried not to shudder as a chill rushed over him.

▲ ▲ ▲

Nathan Webber had not rested since his wife passed away, killed on a narrow stretch of road a mile from home. No other cars involved. A high rate of speed was ruled out. There was no blood-alcohol. Sherry didn't drink. A deer, perhaps, the police offered. She might have fallen asleep. It happens more often than you'd think.

Their attempts at explaining away his wife's death were not comforting. And the knowledge that it happened often was even more distressing.

Especially after he discovered the cross.

It looked handmade, carved from a single piece of hardwood. A simple design, really. Just a cross within a circle——not a plus sign, but a cross. Harmless. Thoughtful, in fact. A heartfelt offering to the memory of his wife.

Like most fatal car accidents, Sherry's coworkers, friends, and family had created a makeshift memorial at the scene, marking her memory with flowers handwritten prayers, and other tokens of their appreciation. It warmed Nathan to see how many lives Sherry had touched. He was thankful for the two years he had been allowed to be her husband; loving her, cherishing her, abbreviated though it was. As a professional photographer, he had taken many pictures of her. They adorned the walls of their apartment. Her smile was the essence of joy. The roadside memorial was so beautiful, he had to photograph it, capture its memory. For Sherry. For himself. It was therapeutic.

But his photographs not only captured a moment in time, they captured a glimpse of what would become a living nightmare. There was an object in the pictures, nearly hidden by all the flowers.

He went back to the scene.

There was a wooden cross nailed to the base of the tree Sherry had hit. Nathan stared at it for a long time. Sherry had not been a religious person. Their wedding was the last time they had seen the inside of a church. But the cross appeared damaged. Its circular edge had been crushed, as if it had been there *before* the accident.

▲ ▲ ▲

The police sirens were wailing again, on their way to another accident. Nathan's heart began to race. He had to beat them there. He had to hurry. Then he opened his eyes and realized it was just his cellphone ringing. Like coming up from beneath a watery undertow, he pulled himself out of a restless sleep and grabbed the phone.

"Hello?"

"Nate, it's Dan. I got that package you sent."

"Dan? Shit." Dan was a good friend of Nathan's, an old college buddy. He worked as a chemist for a biotech company.

"Sorry, Nate, did I wake you? Is this a bad time?"

Nathan looked at the clock. It was 11 AM. He had missed his morning appointment. "No, that's okay. So, did you find out what it's made of?"

Dan laughed. "Nate, the package was empty. Did you forget to put it in the box?"

Nathan sat on the edge of his bed. His head pounded. He didn't want to hear this. He wanted it just to end, have a simple explanation, and then he wouldn't have to think about it anymore.

"I must have forgotten to put it in there. I've had a lot on my mind, lately." He knew damn well he had put it inside the box, wrapped it up tight, sealed the box with strapping tape just to be sure. It couldn't have fallen out.

"No problem, buddy. Just send it again when you get the chance."

"You didn't happen to throw the box away, did you?"

"You want it back?"

"It's just that maybe..." How could he explain this to Dan? *The wooden icon I sent you, it might be invisible?*

"Nate, really, there was nothing in the box. I made sure of it. Is everything okay?"

"Yeah, everything's fine. I just remembered I'm late for an appointment. Thanks, Dan, I'll talk to you later."

Nathan ran his fingers through his hair. He got up and sifted through the stack of printouts by his computer: pages from various websites. One depicted something called The Tree of Knowledge of Good and Evil. "It was of a species that could not be viewed with the naked eye... a tree that is seen only by divine insight and not natural eyesight," the caption read. Another printout was covered with symbols, one of which was circled with a red marker. It was an oblong shape carved from a single piece of wood, surrounding a cross, called a lamen, which supposedly represented the four natural elements: fire, water, air, and earth. There were other printouts, as well, pages on The Cult of the Cross, talismans and amulets, and other topics on the occult and supernatural, which only worked to fuel Nathan's anger and anguish.

He grabbed the stack of papers and threw them into the garbage. *Divine insight. Bullshit!*

He stared at the pictures on his bedroom wall. Interspersed among Sherry's artfully framed photographs were other photos, tacked haphazardly in place. Photos of roadside memorials, each with a red circle drawn around the place where one of those crosses appeared.

He didn't know how or he didn't know why, but somebody was behind all this. Nathan was sure of it.

He looked at his wife's picture. Her smile squeezed his heart.

"I'll find out who did this to you," he told her, tears streaming from his eyes. "I'll find out, if it's the last thing I do."

▲ ▲ ▲

Nathan bought a police scanner.

Over the next six weeks, there were fourteen accidents in the surrounding area, two fatalities. The first was a young man on his way home from a party; the second, a housewife and mother of three, returning from an errand. As a photographer, Nathan was never much interested in tragedy and pathos. There was already too much unhappiness in the world; he figured he didn't need to add to it. He was a portrait photographer. His subjects were people, families—like the family he doubted he would ever have now. Not twisted metal. Not bored policemen, stone-faced coroners, or nervously grinning spectators. And, least of all, not the on-scene spectacle Nathan was witness to, of a husband and wife returning home from a night out to celebrate their twentieth wedding anniversary, arriving upon the scene of an accident only to realize it is their son who lies lifeless beneath a blanket as rescue workers cut his body free from the wreckage. The cries, the wails of injustice, that followed rivaled even the most piercing of sirens.

Two fatalities. Each, Nathan would later discover, initiated by a harmless-looking piece of wood nailed or lodged in place like a divining rod for death and destruction, placed there before any other memorial tributes could gather.

Two fatalities. Two sets of pictures. The second set much like the first, except a different road, a different curve, a different set of faces in the crowd.

Except for one.

A tall, thin figure wearing a long coat and a wide-brimmed hat, standing inconspicuously along the perimeter of the scene. Hands tucked inside his coat pockets, shadows obscuring his features.

Nathan looked at the twin images. He imagined the smile beneath the shadow, the sick glee residing in the man's heart. Like a pyromaniac returning to the scene of the fire he had set.

Nathan had his man. All he had to do now was wait.

▲ ▲ ▲

It was two weeks before the next fatal accident occurred.

Accident? Nathan didn't even know what to call them anymore. Accident sounded too innocuous. Like luck or circumstance. Nathan began to entertain the notion that there were no accidents. Was it an accident when he and Sherry met? Was it an accident that there was a problem at the bank that night and she had to stay a little later than usual to clear it up? Was it an accident that Nathan insisted they change their minds about eating out and instead offered to cook some spaghetti, make a salad, and have it ready by the time she got home?

But she never made it home. And it was three days before Nathan could bring himself to remove the dinner from the kitchen table. The flicker of police lights lit up the night. A gentle rain was falling and the lights danced across the surface of the road. Nathan sat in his car. He turned the volume down on his scanner. "11-80." Police code for a motor vehicle accident: major injuries.

The ambulance pulled away, sirens off. The crowd dispersed—neighbors, strangers returning to their lives, thankful, perhaps, that death chose someone else this night.

Nathan watched as the tall, thin man got into what looked like a rental and drove off.

Nathan followed him. It was 2 AM.

The man drove to a roadside motel a mile outside of town, and pulled in. Nathan pulled into a 24-hour gas station across the street and began filling up his tank. He watched as the man got out of his car. His walk was deliberate, measured, as he climbed the stairs to the second floor balcony and entered his motel room. He didn't even turn to see if anyone was watching. Guilt-free.

Nathan asked the station's attendant if it was okay if he parked in the back of the lot. He told the kid he was a private investigator working on a case. He slipped the boy a twenty and said there would be more if he could convince the other attendants to look the other way. The attendant grinned and grabbed the money.

▲ ▲ ▲

For the next two days, Nathan dined on convenience store snack food. He watched the world come and go. But the rental stayed put. There were times Nathan dozed, and when he woke, the fear would grip him like a pair of cold hands. What if he missed the stranger? It wouldn't take a minute for the man to walk down to his car and disappear, en route to his next victim.

But the car remained in its slot. No sign of the tall, thin man in the long coat.

On the third night, Nathan had his Swiss Army knife in his hand. He was carving the strange symbol, the lamen, into the vinyl dashboard, when he caught a glimpse of his own face in the rearview mirror.

He hadn't showered or shaved in a week. He had been in the same clothes for nearly as long. Was he losing it? Had his wife's death pushed him so far beneath the shadow of grief that nothing else mattered but this silly notion that accidents weren't accidents but some kind of unnatural conspiracy?

Once again, he felt tears storming toward the corners of his eyes, preparing to drown him in an uncontrollable wave of self-recrimination. He looked at the knife, how it gleamed in the artificial glow of the overhead sodium lights. How easy it would be to cut a simple line down each arm and just bleed away into the night. No more pain. No more tears.

There was movement across the street.

Nathan put the knife aside and grabbed his telephoto lens.

The tall, thin man in the long coat had exited his motel room and locked the door behind him. He appeared to pull a watch from his coat pocket to check the time. Nathan zoomed in to get a glimpse of his face, but the man turned and proceeded to his car.

Nathan cleared the debris from his lap and keyed the ignition. It was 11 PM.

▲ ▲ ▲

The man traveled west, away from the city, and onto rural

routes. Town centers came and went, their blinking-light intersections like ghost towns in an endless night. Nathan made sure to keep far enough behind the rental so as not to draw suspicion. Although he doubted the man paid any heed.

The rental turned onto a narrow side road called Breakneck Hill. Nathan shut his headlights off and followed. He kept close, his eyes never losing sight of the rental's red taillights. About a mile in, at the base of a long hill, the rental braked and pulled onto the shoulder. The car angled its headlights toward a large tree. A hundred yards back, Nathan rolled to a stop and cut the engine. He stepped out into the dark. It was after midnight.

Nathan didn't know what he was going to do or say. He watched as the tall, thin man first checked his watch, then methodically went about his business. He was crouched in the tall grass before the tree, bathed in the white glare of the headlights, quietly nailing one of those wooden crosses into place with a small hammer, when Nathan confronted him.

"Why?"

The man turned. His face was no longer obscured by shadow, his features suddenly lit by the high-beam headlights. Nathan was expecting something hideous, malevolent, a human embodiment of pure evil. But this man looked like somebody's kindly old grandfather. His eyes were a soft, innocent blue. Caregiver's eyes.

"Oh, my, you startled me, young man."

"Why?" Nathan asked again. His hands were balled into fists at his side.

The man turned to the wooden icon and gave it a few more taps. He stood up slowly and pocketed the hammer. His expression was unchanged. "You would not understand," he told Nathan.

"Try me." Nathan could barely hang onto reality. This was the man who killed his wife. Why wasn't he at the man's throat choking the life from him?

"Why? Because they wish it so, that's why."

"What is that supposed to mean? Who are *they*?"

"Oh, you don't want to know. Please, accept your loss, move on with your life." The man stared into Nathan's eyes. "But that would be difficult, now, wouldn't it?" He reached into his coat pocket and pulled out his watch. It wasn't a typical pocket watch. It was circular, but it had two dials, each on a different plane. "There's not much time," the man said, "they'll be coming soon." He tucked the watch back into his pocket.

"Please," pleaded Nathan. "My wife. Why her? Why any of them?"

"Oh, it's nothing personal, believe me. I have no knowledge of who will be next. I just know the time and the place. It is very precise, actually. And it provides structure and order to an otherwise chaotic world."

"For whom?" Nathan asked incredulously.

"I'm sorry. For them, of course." The man's arm gestured to some invisible component in the night sky. "You see, the pain, the suffering these events inspire—they hunger for it. Like you and I, they need to be fed. I merely set the table. Do you recall a mother of three who was killed a short time back? Tragic, wasn't it? They could have taken the entire family, but they chose just her. But it wasn't to spare her children. Quite to the contrary. Her children will grieve for *years* to come."

Nathan became enraged. "But isn't there enough pain and suffering in the world without you adding to it?"

The old man laughed, a cheery, good-natured chuckle. "I don't add to it, I merely participate in bringing it about. As the saying goes, it's a nasty job, but somebody has do it." A smile graced his lips. His face was warm and loving. "You see, these beings—these creatures, if you will—I call them grief angels—they are as necessary as the air we breathe. You might think it monstrous, but without the horror and the cruelty and the ugliness that exists throughout the world, there would be no jubilation, no delight, no beauty, and absolutely no hope. Without the one you cannot have the other. Shattered youth, broken innocence, the utter senselessness of untimely death—to them it is all just caviar and cheesecake with a white wine chaser."

"You're insane," spoke Nathan. His voice was weak. It felt like his insides were pouring out.

"No, young man, I am just an ordinary fellow with an extraordinary occupation." Once again, he pulled the strange timepiece from his coat pocket. "Oh my, I really must be going." The man then turned and began to walk back to his car.

Nathan stood on the side of the road questioning everything he had ever believed in. He no longer felt grief stricken. Nothing was going to bring his wife back, he realized that now, and crying about it only fed the bastards who had orchestrated his pain. He wasn't about to stand by, however, and let what had happened to him happen to another husband, or wife or mother and father. The old man had left him with no other option.

Nathan pulled the Swiss Army knife from his pants pocket and pried the wooden icon from the tree.

"Here," he shouted. "Aren't you forgetting something?" He threw the object at the old man. It hit him in the back and fell to his feet.

The man turned. He didn't look angry. In fact, he seemed… *relieved.*

"So, you're the one," he said.

There came the sound of a car racing in the distance. Headlights popped into view over the crown of the hilltop that led down to where the two of them stood. The old man held his ground. Nathan yelled for him to get out of the way. But the car was traveling too fast. The old man turned to face the oncoming vehicle and spread his arms as if to embrace it. The car locked up its brakes. Nathan watched in horror as the vehicle struck the old man, sending him end-over-end into the air and then back down onto the pavement in a shattered heap.

The car skidded to a stop. Nathan rushed to the old man's side, and cradled his head.

"I'm so sorry," he said.

The old man forced a smile. "It's quite all right." He coughed, and his body convulsed. Blood seeped down the corner of his mouth. "It is up to you now," he said. "You must feed them."

Nathan shook his head. "I can't."

The old man's eyes intensified. He grabbed Nathan's arm. "If you don't, there will be chaos." He reached into his pocket and pulled out the timepiece and put it into Nathan's hand. "Now you will truly see."

Nathan felt a strange sensation in the center of his palm as his fingers folded around the circular mechanism. The old man also handed him a set of keys.

"Mister, is he going to be okay?"

Nathan looked up. The teen driver's eyes were shot with adrenalin and fear. But that wasn't the only thing Nathan saw. Behind and above the teen's head, odd shadows were forming. They appeared from out of the darkness like images on photographic paper in a bath of developer—shapeless, diaphanous forms that seemed to grow more substantive as the moments elapsed.

The teen was shaking. Guilt, pain, terror—the essence of each was seeping from his body in multicolored tendrils. The creatures moved in close and began to feed on the dark delicacies.

Nathan returned his attention to the old man. Soft blue eyes stared up at him. The old man's face held a look of peace and contentment. He was no longer breathing.

"Stay with him," Nathan told the teen. "I'll get help." Nathan pocketed the watch and the old man's keys and ran to his car.

▲ ▲ ▲

At the first available payphone, Nathan called in the accident. He then headed back to the motel where the old man had been staying.

The room was sparse. It smelled of old books and onions. Clothes hung on hangers in the closet. The bed was neatly made. On the lamp table lay a book. Nathan sat on the edge of the bed and picked it up.

It was a copy of the Koran. A newspaper clipping was stuffed inside, acting as a bookmark. *Woman Dies in Auto Crash*, the caption read. *Marie Richmond, 26, wife of Tompkin University professor, William Richmond, died early this morning when her automobile plunged into the Tompkin*

Reservoir. The cause of the accident is still under investigation.

The clipping was yellow with age.

Nathan pulled the timepiece from his pocket and examined it in the light. Its housing was made of wood. The two dials appeared to be made of polished crystal, each slightly elliptical. The bottom face indicated a date and time, the top face, a direction. Each dial also had an outer ring that moved independently. Nathan rotated each ring until they aligned. The next alignment would occur in two days. Another fatal accident. Another contribution to the well of pain and suffering in the world.

Nathan wanted to destroy the timepiece, but couldn't bring himself to do it. He could still see Richmond lying in the road, the look of contentment on his face even at the moment of his death. His was a tragic and yet noble life.

Without the one you cannot have the other.

Nathan went to stand, and his heel kicked something beneath the bed. He reached down and pulled out a canvas sack. He uncinched the top. It was full of wooden icons. Enough to last a lifetime.

▲ ▲ ▲

One year later, Nathan watched the homes slide by as he drove out of town and onto the backroads. There was comfort in the knowledge that his actions preserved a sense of balance in his tiny corner of the world. He was sure there were others like him taking care of their own designated space, just as he was sure there were places without a caretaker, places where chaos ruled the night as well as the day.

He checked his watch. The twin dials glowed an ominous yellow in the night. Their alignment was close at hand.

Nathan whistled a nonsense tune as he drove along the empty country road. He couldn't wait to set the table for them. It gave him such pleasure to see them gather.

It gave him such joy to watch them feed.

We switch now to an old-fashioned ghost story. Texas Gothic, as author Jon Black, calls it. Imagine you are sitting on a front porch listening to an old-timer spin this tale, faithful dog and his guitar at his side.

So Lonesome I Could Die
By Jon Black

By day, State Highway 16 between Koenigsburg and Kerrville is one of the prettiest stretches of road in Texas. At night, those same miles become eerie, a corridor of ephemeral shadows where nothing feels real and anything seems possible. Sometimes, on moonlit nights, you'll see a young man walking along the road, thumb out, with a cowboy hat on his head and an old guitar in one hand.

If you stop to give him a lift, you'll notice he's a lanky fellow with lean good looks and an earnest smile. He looks, in fact, a little like Hank Williams. As you drive, he'll say he likes your car and talk about the weather. Then he'll talk about music. But it's probably not the music that you know. Sometimes, he'll tell you he's on his way to a gig that is going to be his big break, and that things are going to turn out just fine for him and his girl. About then you're coming up on a crumbling old brick building outside of Switchbox and he says you can let him off here. Pulling over, you'll hear your car door shut. By the time you glance back, he'll be gone.

But look around outside that old building and you'll find wilted flowers, a small candle, maybe even a guitar pick. Someone remembers.

▲ ▲ ▲

Skim through the index of any history of Texas music and you're unlikely to find an entry for Junzt County. The hottest thing ever to come out of that strangely ancient region of hills and woods where Anglos, Germans, and Native Americans come together was a kid named Johnnie Gruene. In case you're not from around here, that's pronounced "Green" just like the color. More than a handful of decades ago, Johnnie's star burned brightly but briefly and then vanished as suddenly as it appeared.

His father, it was said, had been a traveling man who had won the heart of a local girl with his quick smile. His feet were just as quick, leaving the girl with a broken heart, a broken promise, and, soon afterward, a child to which she had nothing to give but her last name.

People said his father's line was originally from Ireland, and that both magic and madness flowed in their blood. And, it was remembered, the father's father had been a Sooner and that, late at night, during prairie lightning storms, he would stand outside on the hardscrabble earth playing the fiddle. The best damn fiddle playing you ever heard.

His mother's family was from Germany and, though they had fallen among the ranks of the humble, family lore said they had once been Meistersingers and Minnesingers. From the first night Johnnie was in his cradle, his mother sang to him. Though she was seldom around, cleaning the houses of the well-to-do for a few dollars a day, she sang to her son whenever she could.

In Johnnie, the gifts of both those lines were present in the fullest measure. If, while they were still living, you had talked to the right people, they would have told you that the child had sung before he spoke. They would remember it as the voice of an angel, but touched by a melancholy unnatural in one so young. They might also have spoken of his ability to quickly take the measure of any instrument placed in his hand.

The year that Johnnie turned twelve, his mother spent more time at work than ever. Though there was a depression on, she managed to put away a nickel here and a dime there. On Christmas morning, Johnnie found a secondhand Martin six-string, and not much else, under their sparse tree. Johnnie took to that guitar like a duck to water.

Family circumstances being what they were, work was a part of his life almost as early as music. As a child, he spent weekends helping his mother clean houses. From the time he was ten, he did odd jobs for local farmers. It was a close thing, but Johnnie graduated from high school. Afterward, he found steady work at Clay's Garage in Koenigsburg. He was no master mechanic, but he could do enough to justify his paycheck each Friday.

Easygoing as he was, Johnnie got along with everyone at the garage. But he got especially close with two of them. As good as invisible to most folks, Dexter Hawkins, known as Old Dexter, was the simpleminded cleaning man who tidied up the place after everybody else had gone home. Then there was Calvin Clay, another mechanic and son of the garage owner. A couple years older than Johnnie, the two shared a passion for music.

Clay sang and played fiddle, making something of a name for himself around town. After they played together a few times after work, Clay was impressed enough to introduce Johnnie to the friends he made music with. Kermit Mann, serious and sullen, played steel guitar and Dobro. Watt Smith, a natural-born hell-raiser, played standing bass. Sometimes the good-natured Sonny Weidner joined them on accordion.

It was also through Calvin that he met Margarite, a slender, black-haired beauty of the same age as Johnnie. Her family were friends with the Clays and she and Calvin had grown up together.

After joining the group, it was clear that Johnnie offered the musical spark they had been missing. Young people all over were falling in love with the guitar and Johnnie played it better than anyone for 100 miles in any direction. The older folks responded to something in his voice, wild and haunted, like the singers they had known when they were young. Johnnie's guitar slowly pushed the band's fiddle out of the spotlight, even as he was taking lead vocals on more and more of the songs.

The band got busier than ever. Hardly a Friday or Saturday went by when they weren't playing at some school auditorium, house party, or old country dance. Then they started getting gigs at the honky-tonks: Bauer's, Country Creek Bottle House, Eastside Tavern, the Original Gun and Knife Club, the Red Rooster, and Schroeder's Place.

They even brought down the roof at the Yellow Rose Dance-hall. Oh, don't make any mistake, they called it a "dancehall," but it was as rough-and-tumble a honky-tonk as you'd find anywhere in the Hill Country. Old Man Daniels opened the place after coming back from the Great War with lungs full of mustard gas and a head full of shit-house rats. Originally little more than a front for bootlegging, the Yellow Rose occupied an old garage outside of Switchbox, far enough off the beaten path that it was difficult for the authorities to hear about, let alone investigate, every little batch of moonshine, shooting, or stabbing.

When the Feds repealed Prohibition, Old Man Daniels had to go legit. Living by the motto "go big or go home," he built the place into the county's top honky-tonk. Its house band, the Switchbox Six, were infamous for living lives every bit as hard as the ones they sang about, and celebrated for being the county's best band. At least until Johnnie and his crew walked through the door. That night, the Switchbox Six knew they had been put into second place.

Johnnie and his boys had tunes to please any taste: reels, hill-billy music, cowboy music, gospel, Western swing, and Nashville-style country, as well as the newer, faster country that was becoming popular in the honky-tonks. And, whenever Sonny Weidner showed up, they could also play those half-country, half-polka tunes the old German farmers loved so much.

But Johnnie had broad musical horizons. Late some nights, he'd cross over the tracks in Koenigsburg and sit with the old black men outside their homes. He'd play some country and they'd play some blues. Then they'd play some country and he'd play some blues. And they'd all drink whisky and know, whatever separated them, they were all singing about working too hard, drinking too much, finding good women, and losing them again.

Soon, the group came to the attention of KJZT-AM's *Junzt County Barn Dance*. Modeled after the Grand Ole Opry, each Friday the three-hour program featured live performances by the county's top musical acts: Country Tom Boyle, Lottie Dawson, Jean and Johannes, the Koenigsburg Kowboys, John "The Comanche Fiddler" Kutseena, the Ostback Polkateers, and, of course, the Switchbox Six.

Sometimes, the *Barn Dance* brought in guest performers from Austin, Abilene, or San Antone, names like Cliff Bruner, Spade Cooley, Moon Mullican, the Shelton Brothers, and even Bob Wills and His Texas Playboys. But to hear the old folks tell it, Johnnie and his boys put them all to shame, Wills not excepted.

Before long, Johnnie had money. Not a lot, but more than he knew what to do with. A good boy, most of it went to his mother. Now she had nice clothes, a vacuum cleaner—even a washing machine. For himself, Johnnie only took a little. He restrung his old Martin and got some badly needed new duds. His one concession to vanity was a broken-down Ford Slantback, which he worked at restoring when he wasn't on shift at the garage, making music, or spending time with Margarite.

Yes, Margarite. She and Johnnie started spending a lot of time together. Sometimes, Calvin tagged along. Other times, it was just the two of them. Plenty of tongues wagged about the black-haired beauty and gifted music-maker, wondering whether the pair was now "an item."

Fortune just kept smiling on Johnnie. Ralph Peer, a birddog for Victor Records, had caught the boys' performance on *Junzt County*

Barn Dance while on his way to Houston. Driving along the edge of KJZT's signal, he couldn't hear them well. But what he did hear left him wondering if Johnnie wasn't the most exciting thing he'd found since cutting the Bristol Sessions with the Carter Family and Jimmie Rodgers.

Peer wanted to hear more, and arranged a gig for Johnnie and the boys that Saturday night out at the Yellow Rose. He swore, if he liked what he heard then, he'd sign Johnnie to a contract with Victor Records on the spot and turn the kid into the biggest star in Nashville.

That Saturday morning, folks saw Johnnie go down to Ringel's Jewelry on the square. Leaving Ringel's, he went over to Margarite's and the two took a long walk in the woods behind her house. Afterward, he spent a few hours at the garage, whistling happily as he worked on the Slantback. Johnnie's car was nearly ready and he wanted to drive it out to the Yellow Rose for the show. Calvin showed up after a bit and offered to finish up on the car so Johnnie could go home, relax, and get ready for his big night.

It was already dusk when Johnnie returned to the garage and collected his car. Turning the key, he listened to its engine purr for a few moments. Shaking hands with Calvin, who said he had a few things to finish up before leaving for the gig, Johnnie set the old Martin guitar in his passenger seat, got into the car, and drove off. It was a quarter hour more before Old Dexter, pushing his mop through the garage, watched Calvin leave in his Packard convertible—an image, for some reason, he found vaguely troubling in the few years left to him.

Johnnie never made it to the Yellow Rose.

The next day, stopping for gas at the general mercantile in Koenigsburg, Sonny Weidner bumped into Calvin Clay buying a new tire iron and asked him what happened. Calvin said he didn't know. But he added that Ralph Peer, angry at being stood up, had left Junzt County in a huff, vowing never to return.

The old Slantback was soon discovered on Highway 16, about midway between Koenigsburg and Switchbox, near the old Hexencreek Bridge. The hood was up and the driver's door ajar. Days went by, then weeks, but there was no trace of Johnnie. Some folks reckoned he had gone up to Nashville to make it on his own. Others said the call of his father's blood just got too strong and he skipped town for parts unknown.

In June, the *Koenigsburg Zeitung* announced the wedding of Calvin Clay and Margarite. Nine months later a baby was born. Or maybe it wasn't quite nine months. And when some of the old folks looked at that infant, they whispered. Especially the ones who played a bit of music. They knew what a fiddler's eyes looked like. And they knew what a guitarist's eyes looked like too.

Nobody ever saw Johnny Gruene again. And with him vanished Junzt County's chance for musical fame and glory.

▲ ▲ ▲

Yes, by day, State Highway 16 between Koenigsburg and Kerrville is one of the prettiest stretches of road in Texas. At night, those same miles become eerie, a corridor of ephemeral shadows where nothing feels real and anything seems possible. Sometimes, on moonlit nights, you'll see a young man walking along the road, thumb out, with a cowboy hat on his head and an old guitar in one hand.

If you stop to give him a lift, you'll notice he's a lanky fellow with lean good looks and an earnest smile. He looks, in fact, a little like Hank Williams. As you drive, he'll say he likes your car and talk about the weather. Then he'll talk about music. But it's probably not the music that you know. Sometimes, he'll tell you he's on his way to a gig that is going to be his big break, and that things are going to turn out just fine for him and his girl. About then you're coming up on a crumbling old brick building outside of Switchbox and he says you can let him off here. Pulling over, you'll hear your car door shut. By the time you glance back, he's gone.

But look around outside that old building and you'll find wilted flowers, a small candle, maybe even a guitar pick. Someone remembers.

Descanso for November 2016

by Lita Kurth

We were on our way
to a muffled potential
a pressed-down hope
a wilted possibility

I killed my dream with a straight
line between two black squares

Goodbye Bernie. Now I can set up my Descanso
A bumper sticker: *Bernie because fuck this shit.*
A tee shirt: *Thank you, Bernie*

My Descanso will go by the entrance ramp
My Descanso for a rough and rapid end
My Descanso for remembering
what we can't have again. My Descanso
of two point eight million
crosses by the road. Say a prayer for those who don't count
for those who can't count
past two hundred and seventy
Just say a prayer.

*A trip to Chimayo, New Mexico, and a writing challenge,
inspired this fast-paced yet atmospheric piece, from C.A. Cole.
She imbues the piece with the lively, arid atmosphere of the
American Southwest.*

New Mexico State Highway 76
by C.A. Cole

CREMO and me raced through the trees, down the blacktop, riding the centerline, past the descansos, the memorial markers, one a big heart with orange and pink flowers twined around it. It was as huge as a hula-hoop, so big the dead kid could have stepped through it.

Cremo shot on the highs and hit the accelerator down the straight stretch. There was nothing in that dark area but the closed farm stand with ristras rocking in the wind and the side road heading up the hill. That road was so steep, everyone parked and walked. Near the first twist on the slope, three crosses tressed with tinsel glinted in the sun during the day. In the dark, the beams caught a flutter, like hair blowing from the dead woman's head.

Story was, she and her boyfriend had geared down to maneuver that gravel road and had driven right off the first curve, landing on the convertible top. Her hair streamed out the side as if they were cruising in Heaven's slipstream.

I grab Cremo's banded wrist and the cold silver with the knobby turquoise. I stole that bracelet from my dad's tumbledown tourist shop to prove my binding love. I squeeze as if to steal the cuff back from his skinny arm. "Slow down."

The whites of his eyes flick in my direction, and through my hand on his wrist, I can feel his leg slide in his seat, his foot pressing on the accelerator.

"You want to walk?" His voice rumbles like the words are phlegm and I am the spittoon. I withdraw my fingers, leaving the silver to clunk back to his protruding bone.

The high beams catch silvery circles on the side of weathered wood, ghostly white steel poles crossed with fluttering red ribbon. A crucified teddy bear looms on a tall plank, light reflecting off its button eyes. Someone has added seasonal jack-o-lanterns to a grove of white crosses. I know these markers better than I know Cremo's rough fingers. I know their stories.

"Crem," I try again, but white flecks of seething spit dot the dashboard.

I don't want my hair ribbons and plastic pansies to mound against a diminutive cross. I sink back, staring out the window, and watch the byways of my life flash past.

We're flying now. Red slits ahead, a tractor maneuvering after dark. Cremo screeches around it, hits the brake so the tractor light looms in the back window. He slips down the seat again, arms tense, hits go, and we're rocking down the blacktop, slipping through the leaves, on our way to nowhere from no place much.

*We all have our personal rituals and ways of dealing with
grief and loss. Kevin Wetmore's story is a creative take on
that process.*

Burial at Fishkill Creek off I-84

by Kevin Wetmore

THE sky is just turning from blue to ash gray dusk as I start down the
hill on I-84, past the town of Fishkill, the ghost of my ex in the passenger seat next to me. Her absence is a strong presence, as this is the
first time in years I have done this drive without her, and the constant
realization that I am going home alone keeps me in a state of unease.

Entering New York always feels like a transition. There's no
border, no radical change in the landscape. Pretty much looks exactly
the same. But when I pass the Welcome to New York, The Empire
State, Some Guy, Governor sign, well, to a Connecticut Yankee born
and bred, this is always new territory. I'm not in New England anymore, despite the similar view outside the windows. This is not home.
This is New York. It looks the same, but somehow, it's different. I
wonder if it's the same for folks heading east, passing into Danbury
from New York.

The sun is dropping quickly behind the hills to the southeast, the Hudson giving up its glint like a river of gold dissolving into the earth in the cool, September evening light. The leaves are not yet turned, but there is a sense they will soon. It's not summer; it's not fall. It's that time of year when the weather cannot seem to decide what time of year it is. It is beautiful.

The landscape is postcard perfect and I want it all to turn to rot. I turn the radio on and off and yell at the other drivers for driving too slow or too fast or for cutting me off or for not having the balls to cut me off like they so obviously want to. Every passing second a reminder that I am driving the 84 corridor alone.

I pull over to the side of the highway before I hit Beacon to breathe deep and beat the steering wheel, to give voice to my rage in a manner that will not result in an accident. I then take another deep breath, check the rearview mirror, and rejoin the mighty river I-84 as it flows toward the mighty Hudson.

We'd met in college, dated on and off, making it more on than off after graduation and into grad school. Moved in together. Got jobs in Harrisburg, because when you're an academic, home is where the work is. Rachel had degrees in Art History and Business, and so, was able to land a better job than me at a posh art museum in midtown (meaning she got benefits denied the poor adjunct professor—at least, after we got married, I would have health insurance, I figured). I had a Masters in comp, and the only job I could find was teaching freshman writing at Harrisburg Community College. I'd thought things were going good for us. We had been together for six years (a long time when you're in your late twenties) and I had proposed and she had accepted.

A dozen times a year, we took the trip to see my folks in Connecticut, always following the same route. I-81 North to the I-84, then east through New York into Connecticut, my childhood home, then back again at the end of the visit. My folks were older, had had me later in life, and I was an only child, so I wanted to have time with them when I could, and Rae said she didn't mind. So, every third weekend, or the nearest holiday to it, we drove the five hours from Harrisburg to central Connecticut and then back again. It was comfortable. It was good. It's a cliché, but I knew the route like the back of my hand, and I could drive it blindfolded.

What I didn't know was the serial cheating. I learned about some of it along the way—the high school boyfriend she hooked up with when she went home to visit during our first year together. She confessed that one in tears when he texted her and I saw the text. Then there was the guy from grad school, her project partner—"Not-so-single-Bill," she called him. Bill and she had a fling, then she learned he had a fiancée and ended it. Once again, tears and apologies and "I can't believe I did this to you" histrionics to turn her unfaithfulness into a crime against herself somehow, not me.

I know. I'm an idiot.

We were planning the wedding two weeks before when she yelled, "I can't do this!" and walked out. Back in half an hour to tell me she had been secretly dating her boss and was now going to move in with him. She packed up her things and was gone by sundown, leaving me to figure out how I was going to afford our place on an adjunct's salary, and how to break the news to my folks.

In person, as it turns out. After radio silence about it, two weeks later, now, I do the drive from Harrisburg to Connecticut, to see the folks in West Stafford. They are not surprised by the news. Frankly, they seem relieved. Tell me they never liked Rae. It's an awkward visit. Finally, Sunday afternoon arrives. I delay the inevitable long enough, not wanted to drive back alone to my empty apartment in a city I no longer feel my own. I throw my stuff in the trunk of my "previously owned" fifteen-year-old Honda Accord, shake my dad's hand, hug my mom, and kiss her on the cheek.

"Drive safe," she says.

"Well there go my plans for a fun accident," I give my time-worn, not-so-jokey reply.

"Didn't she give you this jacket?" my mom asks casually, but puts enough vinegar behind "she" to let me know exactly how she feels.

"Don'tworrymomI'mfine," I rush the words out together. I breathe. "I'm not going to toss out everything she ever touched. Besides, it's getting cool, and you always tell me to…"

"Fine, fine," she interrupts and repeats, "Drive safe," taking my father's arm in hers.

"See you next month, son," Dad says, and turns away to go back in before I even start the car. Mom will stand on the driveway until I go around the corner and she can't see me anymore.

Ten minutes through West Stafford's late afternoon streets and I am on I-84 with all the other folks headed west. I turn off the radio, as Rae and I would always sing along with the oldies stations (we knew every one from Hartford to Harrisburg). I don't feel like singing.

Rae's ghost is in the passenger seat. I put my phone down there, along with the jacket, so the seat doesn't look empty, but that just makes it more obvious no one is there.

I go through Waterbury, pass Newtown, and hit Danbury, then finally leave the Nutmeg State behind for Terra Incognita. I drive, numb, until I pull off the road to punish the Honda's steering wheel for my sins before rejoining the river.

Then it hits me, I have driven this route every month for the past three-and-a-half years, and I know nothing about it. On an impulse, I pull off at the next rest area, just before Beacon. I jump from the car, use the facilities, and then go to the faded, yellowing pages behind glass on the bulletin boards. Next to the photos of missing children and the highway map, is a brief local history, which is what I was looking for. I study it with newfound purpose. I will make this strange land familiar to me. I will not feel alone and lost along the I-84 corridor through the Hudson Valley on my way between homes.

Beacon, it turns out, is named to commemorate the fires lit on the summit of Fishkill Mountain to alert the Americans about British troop movements. I feel oddly more at home now. You can't turn your head in New England without seeing a plaque about some Revolutionary War event or how the locals helped to defeat the British. I also just like the name "Fishkill." It makes me giggle. I had assumed it was a spot where George Washington slaughtered a large number of fish loyal to England. And "Fishkill Mountain" must be where a whole bunch of fish were slaughtered on the slopes, right? Nope. "Kill," according to the friendly sign posted in the rest area, means "creek" in Dutch. Fish Creek. Kind of obvious, not as cool. I feel let down. Still, I have been given a purpose here. I must actively work to change my life, and it starts here in New York, the place between Connecticut and Pennsylvania, my two homes.

Then I look again at the pictures of missing kids. Some of the fliers just have a picture of a smiling toddler or surly tween. Others have "aged photos" to show what a child missing from seven or eight years ago might look like now. I shiver as I think about the time that has passed and what a hell that must be for the parent who knows the child is out there, maybe even still alive, but now grown into someone else. And this image is not even their photo; it's what a computer thinks they would look like now. I am looking at ghosts, I think. Some of these children are dead, and some are no longer the children in these photos. They are now in the wind, perhaps travelling the river I-84 like I am now, a potholed and cracked Styx that carries them to an underworld, or, worse, a concrete Lethe, the child forgetting who it is and who loved it, as it, gets older and further away from the moment that it was taken from the world in which the original photo was made.

God I'm morbid when depressed. What's next, imagining the children Rae and I might have had, and now realizing they will never be? Time to get back in the car. As I walk away from the children's fliers, I realize that, unlike those parents, I now have answers. I must begin mourning, not hoping reality is different. Time to mourn and move on, as my father dryly noted in the conversation on Friday about my change in relationship status. I begin to think New York is where people from Connecticut go to have emotions.

First things first, I must bury the past. I decide to take this literally. I climb back into the car and turn the engine. I re-enter the highway and decide to follow any impulse that comes into my head. That would have driven Rae crazy, so it seems appropriate as a means to exorcise her.

I get off at the last exit before the Hudson. I have never been here before. Local route 9D takes me from the highway into Beacon. There are fewer cars here. No signal fires on the hills above tonight. The British must have learned their lesson, I think. I must do the same.

I turn right instinctively onto something called Tiorondo Avenue, and see a smaller stream flowing toward the Hudson. Suddenly, I am at something called Madam Brett Park. I decide here is where we hold the funeral. I park the car on the side of the road, grab the jacket, and enter the park. There, in the fading light, I stand on the bank of Fishkill Creek. There was an abundance of rain this past summer, the creek has run high. I drop to my knees next to a tree on the bank that has seen better days and begin to dig with my hands. The tree's branches reach to the sky, but wither and die a half dozen yards up. Clearly other branches have fallen off due to wind or snow. The tree is mostly dead. I clear a space about a foot and a half deep before I start hitting the hard-packed rocky soil. I place the jacket Rae gave me into the hole and, pausing to say goodbye, push the dirt back on top of it and pack it down again with my foot.

Stupid, I know. Nonsense, I know. But somehow, it helps. It feels like I am burying some aspect of our relationship. I giggle again. I am holding a mock funeral for my relationship in a park on the bank of Fishkill Creek (isn't that redundant, my mind absently asks? To any good Dutchman the name means "Fish Creek Creek"—the idle thoughts of a broken-hearted English comp professor).

Standing over the grave of my relationship, I wonder if I should say a few words, or sing something. A song about moving on or being ready for the future, or maybe an angry, metal, you-never-really-loved-me power rant, maybe?

A light rain begins to fall, and I feel like an idiot, trying to decide whether or not to sing something over the buried jacket that would have kept me dry at least.

I realize, though, that I can see the highway crossing the Hudson here. Which means I can see the tree from the highway. Every time

I drive past this point, I will see this mostly dead tree, and know it is where I finally said goodbye to my cheating, lying, fiancée. I also realize that this, too, shall pass. As I shall pass it by. A reminder of pain and loss, and a willingness to keep driving.

Fuck it, I'm not singing here. I'm not spending another minute here. I walk back to the car, climb in, turn the key. I punch the radio up and scan for a contemporary station. A song comes on that is both upbeat and angry. I like it. I push the button that used to mark the oldies station here, and claim that territory now for this station. If I hear something I know, I'll sing along to that.

I follow Tiorondo Avenue back to 9D and then the mighty river I-84. No rushing currents or flotsam and jetsam. Just a flow back toward the empty apartment in Harrisburg. It's a start.

I'll buy a new jacket tomorrow.

My Blood Splatter Analysis of an Alcoholic's Excuse

by Woody Woodger

Figure 2a. shows a passive bloodstain on the hallway
carpet that, in a taste test, was ruled a DNA

match to the sappy chord changes in Lady Antebellum's
latest radio single. Detectives on site found trace

elements of fiberglass and detox shakes in the couch
cushions. A drip trail pattern limped a clubbed

foot across the hardwood, stopped at the fridge.
An intern discovered the dog's blood, piss, and shit

commingled in the excuse's cast-off directed to the year-round
Christmas tree on the side-table. A rubber-glove-shaped

void pattern on the sink handle: inconclusive, possible
projection of evidence. Figure 4d. shows Murphy (dog)

slouched back into himself as a large volume
stain under the coffee table. One commonly overlooked

satellite stain is the air conditioner leaking over the heads
of every silence. Platelets were shucked from his yellowed

beard, burry and scentless. All vocal quivers we tested
turned suddenly bright under luminol. Conclusion: investigation

suggests it is plausible the drunk could persuade the deaf
to comprehend the word *undulate* without ever having heard

how the letters calamari themselves like an excuse the drunk
left misted and unwashable on a loved one's cheek.

*Our next piece is a soldier's powerful memoir of the way a
German airfield and the abuses she suffered there linked her
in silent communion with the victims of atrocities committed
in that place more than half a century before.*

Tatort
by Diana Brown

THE memory of my arrival at the Airfield is vivid and three-dimensional.

The sky was pale, cornflower blue; even that pastel shade looms vibrant and intense. The rumbling of the jet engines as they took off and landed was crisp and distinct, the sound waves disrupting the air around me so intensely that it made my stomach vibrate. The barest of breezes feathered my bangs and swept the sweat from my skin before it could settle there.

The late-summer scent of cabbage hung heavy, so thick that it changed the taste of the air. The Germans let it lie fallow in the fields, waiting for it to reach some delicate point between "overripe" and "rancid" that was, apparently, perfect for the production of kraut.

My emotions were equally sunny and detailed, full of hope, and painted with the conviction that the world is a fine place and life is a grand adventure.

And why not? I was young, and healthy, and my life was perfect! The Army had not only sent me to live in Europe, but had given me the assignment of my dreams. On that day, I could not imagine any way in which my life could be better.

Thirty years later, the memory of that day still registers on all of my senses.

The memory of that night was recorded by only one.

▲ ▲ ▲

On a sunny June day in 1908, Count Ferdinand von Zeppelin's LZ4 took its first flight from a meadow on Filder Plateau. On a stormy day that August, a thunderstorm ripped the tethered craft from its moorings, tumbling it onto its side and across the grassy field. Flames shot out almost instantly as hydrogen fuel ignited. The craft was incinerated.

Sympathetic Germans, excited by this wondrous new technology and awed by the tragedy of its loss, donated over 6 million marks to von Zeppelin's efforts. The count used the money to establish Luftschiffbau-Zeppelin, which began as an airship company and later helped make V-2 rockets for the Nazis.

It seems that exalted beginnings and excruciating outcomes are combined in the place's very DNA.

▲ ▲ ▲

I don't remember what it *felt* like; I don't remember *feeling* it at all, even while it was happening. I don't recall the taste of my mouth or the smell of the room. Words were spoken, and I remember them—but I can't recall the *sound* of the conversation. My only memories of those moments are visual. The light is dim, the colors muted, but the detail is crisp, his face distinct.

A prosecutor willing to pursue a rape case is even more rare in the military than it is in civilian life—but our JAG thought the case was strong enough to prosecute. And that was *before* the second victim came forward. And *that* was before they discovered he had been stealing from the government.

He was never convicted, of course—he didn't even bother to attend his own hearing. They waited two hours for him to turn up, or for someone to locate him, then just canceled it. They gave him an honorable discharge and sent him home.

I, on the other hand, was sternly punished for my crimes: embarrassing the unit by drawing negative attention to the command, potentially endangering the commander's promotion, being raped. For the next two years, I served my sentence.

▲ ▲ ▲

In 1936, the Germans built an airfield on Filder Plateau. During World War II, its grass runway served Luftwaffe elites: night fighters and the school where accomplished flyers learned to become glider-towing pilots.

In 1943, a concrete runway was added. Within a year, the Allies were conducting almost nightly bombing runs, shattering the concrete and demolishing the sod as their ground troops marched inexorably into Germany.

In the winter of 1944, somewhere between 600 and 750 Jewish "workers" were brought to the Airfield, among them Mayer Hersh. Taken by the Nazis at the age of 13, Hersh spent over five years in as many as nine different camps, including Auschwitz. His interviews paint a dismal picture of that winter on the Airfield.

The captives were housed in a single hangar whose doors did not close properly, leaving bunks dusted with snow. Some prisoners were tasked with filling in craters and carrying away debris to restore the runways. The rest were sent to the nearby quarry, working in temperatures so cold that the explosives used to break loose the stone often failed to ignite properly. Within eight weeks, more than half of the prisoners were dead.

▲ ▲ ▲

The vile rumors, lurid commentary, and harassing asides were, I am sure, no different than what any rape victim experiences if she is foolish enough to report the crime. I wonder how many of those women find themselves in their boss's office, listening to him threaten to prosecute them for their imagined (and demonstrably fictional) erotic exploits?

The commander explained with stern glee how his promotion had enhanced his capacity to punish and even imprison me for my rumored behaviors. He outlined each imagined crime, detailing the penalties he could choose to inflict. He didn't follow through on those threats, choosing instead to make my life miserable in smaller and continual ways, but his ire made me a fair target for any other sadist or bully who needed entertainment. They knew they wouldn't be punished, and I wouldn't be believed. I was fortunate; the abuse rarely escalated to physical harm.

The Airfield became my prison.

I buried myself in work, reminding myself that in the military, it was performance that mattered. That in a few years, I would leave the Airfield behind, carrying only my excellence with me.

The rumors had travelled across Germany and reached the far side of the Atlantic before they ever scheduled the hearing. No amount of professionalism or dedication could drown them out. As long as I remained in the service, there would be no escape.

▲ ▲ ▲

Within two months of their arrival, more than half of the prisoners died from starvation, disease, beatings, and grueling physical labor. Those unfortunate enough to have gold teeth were clubbed to death by avaricious guards. As the calendar turned to 1945, a typhus outbreak forced the closure of the camp.

Within weeks, the French Army swept through and liberated the region. Within months, Hitler was dead, and the war was over. Before the end of the year, 66 bodies were found in a mass grave in the nearby woods.

Of the 600–750 prisoners brought to the Airfield, only 64 are known to have survived.

We will likely never know how most of them died—how many were beaten to a mercifully-swift death; how many perished slowly of disease; how many were executed in the face of the Allied advance, to prevent their escape or liberation and to silence their testimony.

I can't imagine the Airfield killing someone quickly and mercifully. In my imagination, their demise is like mine—the slow and torturous effect of neglect and dehumanization.

▲ ▲ ▲

My life is divided into "Before" and "After" by the years I spent on the Airfield.

After, I was able to build a reasonably successful life. I left the military, of course, and went to work in technology. Logic and determination were enough to create success, and it was *expected* that I'd be introverted and uncomfortable with people. PTSD could be left entirely out of the conversation.

On the rare occasions when I talk about my military days, I tell tales from Before. I don't talk about Europe, and people generally assume that my stories from that time are classified, so they don't ask.

After, my memories are two-dimensional. Most of them involve more than one sense, but never *all* of my senses. My memories have never again been painted in the vibrant and dazzling palette of "Before."

You know how memories can be—one leads to another, which leads to another. I find it best just not to think of it if I can avoid it.

Sometimes, I am left with no choice. The Airfield forces its way into my thoughts, commandeering my attention. When that happens, I try to think of the *place*—the immaculately-faded roads and buildings, the dull blacks and grays of the aircraft. Leaving the people out of the picture lets me think of it as just a place where I once lived.

When I think about the people, I am forced to remember that it is also the place where my soul died.

▲ ▲ ▲

A decade or so ago, the Airfield gained international attention when a construction project unearthed a shallow grave bearing the bodies of nearly three dozen more prisoners.

Construction stopped, and a swarm of investigators appeared amongst a scattering of *Tatort* (Crime Scene) signs.

Most of the dead appeared to have perished from starvation and disease, but a few had clearly been murdered. Eager to dispose of the evidence, the Germans did not wait for the last prisoners to die before burying them. Perhaps the skulls with bullet holes in them had been viewed as mercy killings by those who pulled the trigger.

The signs came down, the bodies were reburied as close as possible to where they had been found, and dark stones were laid atop their graves.

A memorial was added outside the gates. It's designed in two straight lines, laid out like a runway so that they cross near one end. They are aligned so that one points toward the hangar, the other toward the gravesite. The "runway" aligned to the gravesite is adorned with a long white wall marked *Wege der Erinnerung*—Path of Remembrance.

▲ ▲ ▲

When satellite photos and mapping websites started to become common, I went looking for pictures of the Airfield, intending to show my husband the place where I had lived. When I searched, the first thing I found was the previous year's news articles about the discovery of 34 bodies. It was then that I learned of the Airfield's history.

The photos were innocuous enough——construction-turned earth, investigators kneeling next to *Tatort* signs, a few unidentifiable buildings in the distance. Well, unidentifiable to most people. For me, those blurred outlines marked the spot as clearly as a flare.

I used to do PT on that field.

Had I lain in the dirt, cursing my way through sit-ups, three feet above some innocent person's unmarked grave? Had I dripped sweat on the dirt, my nose inches above the earth while doing push-ups, unaware of the abandoned, thrown-away person buried an arm's length beneath me?

Had I unknowingly treated them with the same heedless

contempt that my comrades-in-arms had heaped upon me?

I didn't show the pictures to my husband; I just stared at them for what felt like hours, without knowing why. These lost souls' experiences at the Airfield seemed connected to my own, and I felt small and arrogant for daring to compare myself to them. Their suffering was so much greater.

Or at least, propriety tells me that is what I should believe.

The camp was only active for three months. Sometime in those 90 days, the prisoners' souls escaped, leaving their unfeeling remains behind. Sometime in the two years I spent on the Airfield, my soul departed, but it didn't escape. It buried itself in the frozen earth, becoming a part of that place, and I have lived on for three more decades without it.

They suffered intensely and swiftly. I suffered less, and for longer. How do you calculate Total Anguish to judge whose torment is greater?

I stared at the images until I found my answer. I acknowledged the dreadful suffering of the dead, knowing that what they experienced was beyond my understanding. I came to think of them as my fellow victims: people abused, neglected, dehumanized, and thrown away by the Airfield. Losses that were meaningless and unnoticed by those who caused them, incalculable to those who suffered them.

I embraced them as kin—the sort of family that is cobbled together from shared suffering. When I did, I began to hear what they had come to tell me.

Through them, I learned that for as long as it had existed, the Airfield had been a place where the vulnerable were abused and worn down until at last they were destroyed.

I learned it had been 50 years from the discovery of the first mass grave to the erection of the first memorial. It was only a few months this second time. The Airfield was slowly learning to acknowledge its transgressions.

I learned that during the war, locals from the surrounding towns tried to help the prisoners, slipping them food and—possibly just as importantly—showing them that someone cared. I wondered if the kindness of the locals had been enough to give the prisoners hope, or if the Airfield had robbed the prisoners of that, as it had me.

I haven't learned to forgive those who abused or harmed or threatened me. I don't know that I *can* forgive those among my "band of brothers" who chose to mistreat me when I most needed them to have my back.

But I have forgiven the ones who stood aside, the ones who chose not to see, the ones who chose not to believe, the ones who chose not to get involved. The ones who were oblivious to how their complicity enabled the rest. I cannot pardon those who were intentionally cruel, but I have been able to forgive the ones who were willing to let me die of neglect.

I am able to turn my back, as they did, and it is sufficient.

▲ ▲ ▲

The wall of the memorial has a break in it, to allow the connecting "runway" to travel through. It seems right to me that this monument should have a gap in the middle, a space for those victims of the Airfield who will remain forever unrecognized and unacknowledged.

I will return to the Airfield one day. I will show my husband the place where I lived. On each of the black gravestones, I will leave a small, white rock, paying respects to my unexpected kin in accordance with their custom.

And when I visit the Path of Remembrance, I will stand in the gap in the wall.

Tin-Tree Descanso

by Teressa Rose Ezell

It took three days to walk there.
When we arrived, the heat
melted pebbles under your
shoes and your tears
made pock-marks in the
thick red dirt.

A man—just a speck—
runs toward us swinging
a ratty blue shirt
stained white from
cleaning, barreling down
the narrow road as if he knows,
as if he knew you.

You counted stars by tens
through cedar branches,
laughed at the sun hiding,
sang with pipe and barred
owl. And then, smack-dab—
just in the very eye-hole
center of nowhere—the
laughter stopped, singing
silenced, an eternal pause

Waiting…

A feather-pipe swings wild
on twisted metal crazed tree
bedecked with a thousand ribbons,
every color flying,
as if calling
you home.

Poetic, erotic, and profound, our next piece, by Jonathan Ochoco, brings us a bittersweet story of love and remembrance, humor, and liberation.

Waiting by the Window
by Jonathan Ochoco

I NEVER believed in ghosts until I saw disco singer Sylvester fucking Oscar Wilde on top of the counter at the Twin Peaks bar.

I see them going at it again when I walk in. Jerry, the bartender, gives me a wave and smile from the behind the bar as I take my usual seat on the orange-cushioned bench by the window. Oscar's hair flops around while Sylvester takes him from behind. I blush and feel like a prude even though I know I shouldn't. It's certainly not the first time I've seen fucking, let alone Sylvester and Oscar doing it. Ever since San Francisco installed bronze plaques for famous gays and lesbians on the sidewalks for the Rainbow Honor Walk, I have seen Sylvester and Oscar every time I've come into Twin Peaks. And I now see the ghosts of all the honorees cruising the Castro.

The first time I saw Oscar and Sylvester going at it, I didn't know what to think. I was sure that senility had finally set in or at least that I'd had way too many martinis. I remember looking around with my jaw hanging open to see if anyone else had seen. But everyone in the bar was lost in their own conversations or staring at their phones. I couldn't believe that bar full of gay men wasn't watching the live sex show. Jerry had been watching me, and I could tell from his raised eyebrows that he had seen the panic on my face. I remember shutting my eyes, hoping it was all my horny imagination after years of self-imposed celibacy, but Sylvester never let up on Oscar's ass. Oscar's squeals grew higher than any note Sylvester ever sang on "You Make Me Feel." I could tell Oscar was definitely feeling something mighty real.

Jerry walks over to my table and sets down one Absolut martini with three olives in front of me before taking a seat and setting a second martini with two olives in front of him.

I try to ignore the show behind Jerry, and give him a weak smile. "Thanks, sweetie."

"Hi Maurice," he says. "Brought you the usual. One for you and one for Bruce, if he comes." Jerry turns to the bar and then looks back to me, his eyes narrowing. "They're here again?"

"Every day. Oscar can't seem to get enough."

"If I were dead and Oscar Wilde, I think wouldn't be able to get enough either." He tilts his head and arches an eyebrow.

I'm itching to respond with scathing sarcasm, but I'm distracted by Oscar and Sylvester's new, contorted position. I focus my attention instead on Jerry's hair, which is now grayer than when I first met him, forty-something years ago, and my own blond hair has long gone. Jerry's arms, though, are as massive as ever. "Still working out I see."

"Not the kind of workouts I really want," he says, winking at me.

I roll my eyes. "What about that twenty-year-old twink from Nebraska?"

"You mean my Tuesday nights?" He laughs that bear of a laugh he has, the one that I used to hear when I would stand outside the bar, too afraid to go in.

I smile and lower my head for a moment, thinking about Bruce. I look Jerry in the eyes, about to respond, when Oscar screams so loudly I think all of the windows will shatter.

I try to suppress a laugh and my eyes water, trying to keep the laughter contained, until I can't keep it in and double over in hysterics. Jerry rolls his eyes. "Is it me? Is my fly open?"

I look at Oscar, now sprawled naked along the bar. Sylvester is sitting next to him in a purple, sequined jumpsuit, dangling a cigarette from his lips and crossing and uncrossing his legs over Oscar's head.

A group of silver daddies walks in. Jerry gets up. "Duty calls." He blows me a kiss.

I take a sip of my martini, feeling the warmth of the vodka slide down my throat. I take a bite of one of the olives. Oscar now sits in a suit, smoking a cigar, with his legs spread open and a bar patron unknowingly sets his beer down in front of his crotch.

I stare at Oscar and think about how Bruce would get such a kick out of seeing those ghosts. He would want to discuss books and politics with James Baldwin, who mostly sat on a ladder at the new bookstore that used to be A Different Light. Or maybe he would want to discuss art and poetry with Frida Kahlo and Virginia Woolf, who are always making out and groping each other in the balcony of the Castro Theatre.

I take another sip and another bite of olive. I gaze at the second glass on my table and picture Bruce holding it just like on the day when we first met. I had been sitting in this same spot, staring out the window, cruising whoever walked by. Bruce had stopped to smoke a cigarette in front of me on the other side of the window, and I couldn't stop staring at his ass in his tight, faded Levi's. When he turned around, I knew he wasn't wearing underwear. I must have been obviously staring because Bruce rapped at the window. I blushed and turned away. Bruce, with his dark, feathered hair and green eyes, strode right in and sat across from me and ordered us martinis, his with two olives and mine with three.

"Liked what you saw?" Bruce said. His eyes twinkled.

I didn't know what to say.

He pressed his boot against my crotch. "Yup, you definitely liked what you saw."

We had more martinis, and dinner, and dessert at his place. I think I screamed louder than Oscar Wilde that night.

I smile at the memory and sigh. I gulp down the rest my martini and watch Oscar and Sylvester giving each other hickeys in the back corner under the stairs leading to the balcony.

I scan the room and see only a few men without white hair or at least hair that isn't glued on. I think of how bold it once was for us to be seen in this bar, where the sun actually shone inside, instead of the other gay bars, which looked like basements. I think about how Oscar never had the option of coming to a bar full of windows.

A smattering of younger men stand at the bar, looking for a daddy, I surmise. But I don't see the face I want to see.

I stare out the window and let the sun warm my liver-spotted and wrinkled face. Tight asses in tight jeans walk by, but none are the ass I'm hoping to see.

Jerry stares at me from the bar with wide eyes, a questioning look on his face. He shakes his head. I shake my head back.

I was surprised that Jerry didn't think I was crazy when I told him about the ghosts in his bar. He's been such a good friend all these years. I pull the toothpick of olives out of the other martini glass and take both of them into my mouth.

I stand up and wave to Jerry as I walk outside. I walk down Castro Street, past some of the Rainbow Honor plaques, trying not to step on the faces of Virginia Woolf, Tennessee Williams, and Oscar Wilde. I turn onto 18th Street, past plaques for Alan Turing and Allen Ginsburg. I turn up Collingwood Street. As I get closer to my house, I stop in front of a magnolia tree just starting to blossom. I stoop down in front of a much smaller bronze plaque that reads "Bruce Davis, beloved husband of Maurice Craig, 1944–2012."

I kiss my fingers and press them against the plaque, and whisper, "Maybe you'll come tomorrow, sweetie. Maybe tomorrow."

Our next story, by Nick Bouchard, uses poetic repetition to set up a rhythm that drives the narrative and carries the story deep into the realm of terror.

The Tall Man
by Nick Bouchard

The rabbit lay in the middle of the street. I saw it hop one last time after being struck. The final hop was just as much habit as it was momentum. It toppled to its side.

The rabbit lay in the middle of the street. Its legs still moved, trying to hop. The front legs made their customary small circles. The hind legs made less graceful, twitchy arcs. It moved like my dog when he dreams. That may have been the toughest part. Road kills happen. But they don't usually keep moving. The rabbit's twitches were so like my Franco's dream-induced strides that I was sure I faintly heard the panting and chuffing sounds that invariably accompanied his dreams.

The rabbit lay in the middle of the street imitating my dog at nap time. I looked to be sure Franco wasn't actually dreaming his dream of canine conquest. He was not. He was at the back door, looking out into the woods. He wagged his tail in lazy sweeps.

The rabbit lay in the middle of the street. And because his final, valiant effort had landed him directly on the double yellow line, he was not dead yet. Had he fallen where he was struck, he would have been finished off by another car. Since folks weren't in the habit of driving on the double yellow, he got to continue his sleeping dog imitation for his meager audience.

The rabbit lay in the middle of the street. I wondered where road kills go. I had seen crows pecking pieces off of them sometimes. Once I saw a skunk lug a meaty strip of raccoon into the trees beside the road. And I had heard a couple stories from people whose pets had been hit by cars. They talked about wrapping their friends in a warm blanket and taking them, motionless, to the emergency vet. None of those stories ended with survival. But I'm sure some must.

The rabbit lay in the middle of the street, still kicking. He showed no signs of slowing. If it weren't for the blob of entrails protruding from his mouth, I might have believed he was just knocked out, dreaming of chasing something. Perhaps he was dreaming.

The rabbit lay in the middle of the street, and I don't know how long I watched, fascinated by his relentless attempt to finish crossing. It could have been minutes. It could have been days. I was so mesmerized, I might not have noted the sun setting or rising.

The rabbit lay in the middle of the street, and a long, old gray car pulled to the side of the road. The door opened, and from behind tinted glass, stood a man. He must have been seven feet tall. He was dressed in a gray suit with dark pinstripes. He reached back into the car, and extracted a bowler hat—which he crammed down over wild yellow hair—and a large valise.

The rabbit lay in the middle of the street, and the tall man looked both ways before moving ponderously toward the center of the road. Rickety as an old split rail fence, he walked with the tentative care of a man on stilts. When he reached the rabbit, he knelt at its side and placed his bag on the ground beside him.

The rabbit lay in the middle of the street, still twitching his fruitless getaway, as the tall man carefully opened his battered valise.

The bag swallowed his forearm as he rummaged for the proper instrument. He drew the length of his arm from the bag to reveal a hammer. The tall man drew his arm back and brought the hammer down on the rabbit's head, striking three swift, precise blows. The rabbit lay still. The man used an enormous thumb to wipe the head of the hammer clean. He returned it to the valise.

The rabbit lay motionless on the road. This time the man reached beyond his elbow into the seemingly bottomless bag. He pulled out a large, pale ring. A roll of masking tape. He reached back into his impossible satchel and produced a large square of gleaming white paper.

The rabbit lay motionless on the large white square. The tall man had placed him there—near the center. Then he picked up one corner of the square and folded it over the rabbit. Then he folded the two sides in and rolled the rabbit out of sight with the care of a mother swaddling her baby. He secured the final corner of the paper wrapping with a piece of masking tape and returned the roll to the bag.

The rabbit lay in the middle of the road, wrapped like a cut of beef on the butcher's scale, as the tall man licked his fingers clean. He picked up his satchel and his grisly papoose. After a few steps, he stopped, turned, and looked right at me. He smiled—and even from that distance, I could see that his teeth weren't normal. Shark teeth. The smile faded, covering the jagged teeth, and he nodded to me just once before getting in his car and driving away. The unsettling smile. The terrifying nod. They said, I see you. I know you see me. Worst of all, they said, you're next.

But I wasn't next. For years, I saw that tall man, with his doctor's satchel, stopping on the side of the road. Have you ever seen him? I sure hope not. I don't think most people can. I don't think people are supposed to see him. He only stops for the ones that still have signs of life: a heaving chest; a blinking, staring eye; gnashing teeth; dreamily kicking legs. You're sure you've never seen him?

Now, here I lie in the middle of the street, staring up at a darkening sky. I could feel the handlebars when they punched into my chest. I felt my knees strike the grillwork. I felt my face hit the wind-shield. I can't feel any of that now. But I remember the smell of beer was thick in the air as I hurtled past the shocked yet sedated face of the driver. His expression was that of someone awakened to find that they were no longer next to the person they had fallen asleep beside.

I lie on my back in the middle of the street. I can't move, and I can no longer feel my injuries. But I can still see and smell and hear. My ears remember the screeching tires. My nose remembers the waft of cheap beer. My eyes remember that rabbit, and I'm not surprised when I hear the throaty rumble of an old V8 by the roadside. Its tires crunch to a stop on the shoulder. The sound of the tires is a slow replay of the sound that came from the base of my skull when I hit the windshield.

I'm lying on my back in the middle of the street, and some-thing tells me that the double yellow is right beneath me. I imagine myself from above. The stripes enter one crippled shoulder and exit at the hip on the opposite side. I hear the door of the old sedan snick open and I hear the springs sigh as someone exits, relieving them of their burden. There is a moment of silence. I hear my pulse quickening in my ears. I know he's putting on his hat and retrieving his satchel.

I'm lying on my back in the middle of the street, and I know there's some outward sign I'm alive because he's here. This could be death, but I know it's not, or he would not be visiting me.

I'm lying on my back in the middle of the street, my pulse is rapidly ticking my life away. The door thunks shut with the satisfying sound big American cars made in the late sixties. I count four uneven footsteps before I see his silhouette, like a skyscraper looming above me. I can see his valise as he kneels, setting it beside my head. Up close, I see that his suit is perfectly pressed. It's clean and looks brand new, even though he's had it for at least twenty years. The suit, as much as the man, has held mythical status for me since that afternoon when I was twelve and home alone while my mother made a grocery run.

Lying on my back in the middle of the street, I see him close-up as he leans over me. His face contorts with something that might pass for a smile. The smile is a slack maw crowded with row upon row of sharp, serrated teeth. One bite could turn steak to hamburger. A rumbling and somehow gleeful sound boils in his throat. His breath is an open sewer and rotting flesh and sulfurous coals. But his face is not what I thought. His face is just a mask. He seems to have the poorly preserved skin of a person pulled over his head. The eyes in those tattered sockets are as shark-like as his teeth, glittering black orbs, infinite and unblinking. There are a few small, circular scars on the face, about the size of a quarter. Small, clumsy stitches wreath each scar. In an instant I realize that the stitching is holding in place the pieces that were punched out by his hammer. The skin of the nose hangs loose. There is nothing behind it to fill out that little pouch of flesh.

I'm looking up at the sky in the middle of the street. His face has disappeared from my vision, and I know he is up to his elbow in that old doctor's bag. He makes another wet, foul-smelling sound of triumph and I know he has found what he's looking for. And I try to close my eyes against the swiftly arcing hammer, but they won't close and the hammer comes down once, twice, three times. I lose count at five. Each blow is more squelchy and less crunchy, until there is only darkness.

I'm lying in the darkness in the middle of the road, and I imagine the tall man, in his tattered man-mask, licking lumpy gray bits of my brain from his fingers. Perhaps a tuft of hair or a stringy gobbet of flesh have snagged in his rows of teeth. I sense nothing, but I know I'll be wrapped in that bone-white paper, that he's up to his shoulder in his satchel, searching for a piece big enough for a grown man. In the darkness, I wonder if I am with my body, being rolled into that paper, like a market-fresh fish. I feel certain that whatever it is that makes me *me* would be lost if it were no more than the contents of my skull, now splashed across the pavement.

Sometimes a simple twist of the wheel is all it takes.
Fred Zackel's uniquely formatted flash piece
When You Least Expect It, a Jackrabbit is a fast-paced
exploration of the sacrifices working people are
forced to make on the altar of their livelihoods.

When You Least Expect It, A Jackrabbit

By Fred Zackel

Por donde menos se piensa, salta la liebre**

My grandfather came up from Chiapas first,
and then he sent for his family. When my grandmother,
my aunts and my father got here in Matamoros,
my grandfather still didn't speak the locals' Spanish, but
he got a job as a trucker. My grandfather was a lonely man,
a melancholic man who had a family to support and nowhere else to
turn. He had hair on his balls, his buddies said, and a short life facing
him. His days were shortened because he could tell no one all the shit
he faced, because he would lose his job if he told. He stabbed his
cigarette out in his food because he lost his appetite too often and
because his future sickened him. Sudden death
on the road scared him the most. He would come home

with pains in his forearms from another white-knuckle ride. The
stiffness in the ankles twisted him, and he'd twist back as hard, as if
opening a rusted jar lid, to get the circulation back. He had strain in
his calves from his legs being so stiff with fear for so long, and the
small of his back was a knot no sword could cut. He was almost
paralyzed by fear after work, and dreaded the next day and its
monsters. His hands wouldn't stop trembling. He drank
because the bottle felt like part of his hand. He drank
because he had phantom pains— real phantoms
that haunted him in the night and brought him
grievous pain. No one knows how it started. No one
ever came forward. But on a warm Sunday, after midnight, he was
on his own, outside Piedras Negras, coming home, as sheets of
white rain plummeted to earth. Then:
somehow the steering wheel ripped loose from his hand.
The tractor flinched, the back lurched and straightened and then fish-
tailed, the tractor now at a right angle to the trailer. The tractor tried
a one-eighty, twisted itself, and landed on its side. The trailer hurtled
past, then jerked the tractor, pulled it along.
The tractor slid down the highway, on its side, the driver's side.
Foot-long sparks shot out bright flashes. The sound was shrill and
loud, like peacocks being tortured. The tractor was sandpapered by
the surface of the road. On its belly sliding into third, sparks the size
of our hands flying out, sparklers in the night
under the stars, skittered down the grade,
sometimes gravel and sometimes asphalt,
the steel rail snapping like a long bone, then the rig snapped
and the cargo shifted. The cab became a tip of a whip getting
cracked. A helpless man became shrapnel. Flesh got skinned and then
got shredded by pavement. He kissed the rocks
on a summer night. He died because of the whiskey and the
cigarettes and the other poisons he put in his body to keep going.
He died because of what he ate day in and day out because he had no
real choice or opportunity to eat any better. He died

because he was too scared to see a doctor
because the doctor might say he couldn't go to work.
He died because his equipment wasn't as good as he wished it was.
He died because he worked surrounded by lunatics and outlaws,
and he always swore up and down that
they were going to get him killed,
by the god above us all. He died because his bosses didn't care, and
he was invisible. He died because his body ached and he was
too tired to move out of pain's way, because he made an honest
mistake and let down his guard, and he couldn't react fast enough,
and because his momentum scraped his flesh off his bones, and his
face off his skull. When the eighteen-wheeler slowed,
the noises faded. No one saw him. He lay silent,
bleeding, a smear on the highway. No one stopped. No one came
forward. Eight hours to bleed out, said the coroner.
Driver error, said the trucking company.
Operator error, said the insurance company.
He died because he thought he could do it one more time,
and this time was his turn.

**"When you least expect it, a jackrabbit pops up."

Desesperanza
by Dave Holt

"Tucson, Arizona. Great town," I say.
That's where she's from. She drops her jumble
of memories on my toes, epic night drives
through "scary Indian reservations"—
Tohono O'odham, Navajo, Pascua Yaqui;
the dangers—real enough, the flower of native youth
laid low, early graves in the desert, markers placed close
to a ditch where the car skidded, spun, rolled, hit a pole,
flared like a Roman candle, flamed out, guttered,
like our Walnut Creek, California, Wonder Bread kids,
who also die in reckless cars.

Two cast-off pieces of wood painted white, one nail
makes a cross, with garlands, tinsel, notes pinned,
a sign—"We love you" (a name), Mason jars
of plastic flowers, graced by candles kept lit
in early weeks, then wayward trash clusters
at the foot of the fragile frame, wind-whipped
monument to mark the place where something
momentous passed—Mother's dream, Father's hope,
a younger brother, or sister's inspiration,
descansos they're called in the Mexican tongue.

Desesperanza, "too much boredom and alcohol," she says.
Despair, self-loathing, desperation roams the star-scaped desert.
Screech of rez cars slamming brakes, moonlit highways
lined with lost hubcaps, junkers, ragged rubber
curled like corpses of black dogs. Farther off the road,
the distant but homey glimmer of hogans,
"squalid shacks," as she calls 'em.

Now she finds a benediction to conclude the sermon…
"If these people had Jesus…" Oh, I don't doubt he helps some.
Sweat lodges, vision fasts, talk circles for others. My prayer is
they awaken to Indian power, the *Yei-bi-chei* in themselves.

Let's get out of this night. Leave her bitter Dixie Cup
there on the asphalt by the roadside descanso,
a zinnia in the Styrofoam, some Crystal Geyser,
a sign on the road to nowhere. We'll follow
a whiff of tire smoke in the dark, spiral of stars
flung like a curtain, an unrolled map,
a constellation, the drinking gourd, etched in light.
corralled dark, cool water out of parched land.

In this next memoir Nicole Scherer reminds us that grief and loss are not only reserved for the loss of living things, as she says a last goodbye to her Navy helicopter.

Last Flight Out
by Nicole Scherer

WE landed from a hover and taxied for what seemed like miles across the desert airfield. At last, the plane captain waved us to a stop, and we began our shutdown procedures inside the cockpit of the Sikorsky SH-60B Seahawk. I held the controls while my copilot ran the checklist and flipped switches. He reached the step that reads, "PCLs – Idle," which directs the pilot to pull the power control levers aft out of the "Fly" detent. "Killing One," he said, indicating that he was securing the Number One Engine. Poor word choice, I thought, as her turboshaft wound down. The Turbine Gas Temperature gauge on both engines ticked to zero, the helicopter's heartbeat flatlining for good.

▲ ▲ ▲

It was late November of 2012. Our final stop on this cross-country flight—accompanied by another due-for-decommissioning SH-60B—was Davis-Monthan AFB, home to the 309th Aerospace Maintenance and Regeneration Group. Pilots call it "the boneyard," a usually final resting place for more than 4,400 aircraft, most of them military. This is Arlington for faithful steel giants who have spent their "lives" in service to their nation. After three decades of salt spray and pitching waves, this dustbowl surrounded by mountains seemed a strange landscape for Navy aircraft. But it would be the final resting place for every SH-60B I had flown in my first three years as a Navy pilot.

I engaged the rotor brake, bringing the blades to stop at the forty-five-degree position off the nose. The sudden absence of the rotor blades' staccato roar made the silence in the cockpit feel just as loud somehow. In just a few seconds, the boneyard workers would surround the aircraft, inspect it carefully, and begin the preservation process. Some aircraft are marked for metal scrap, some are cannibalized for parts to keep other aircraft flying; others are marketed for foreign military sales. A lucky few even return to flight status as the need arises.

I didn't know my aircraft's ultimate fate. I knew that within a period of days, if not hours, she would be drained of all fluids and sealed with a white latex layer called Spraylat. I knew her rotor blades would be removed, giving the aircraft an appearance as unsettling to me as a headless Barbie doll. The lines of Earthbound birds sprawled across the landscape made me think of broken children's toys.

Before unstrapping and climbing out, I reached for the rotary dial of the TACAN, our primary navigation system. I clicked until the numbers read "51X"—the homing beacon channel for Naval Station Mayport in Jacksonville, Florida. Silly, but it made me feel better. *Just in case she ever needs to find her way home.*

▲ ▲ ▲

The Mayport, Florida, squadron I joined in 2010 as a "nugget" aviator sent detachments of six or seven pilots, twenty-odd enlisted maintainers, and one or two helicopters, to deploy on the Navy's smallest boats. Most people assume Navy pilots deploy on aircraft carriers, but the world of the 60B was much smaller than that behemoth of American technology and military might. The USS *Anzio,* a guided-missile cruiser and the largest class of the Navy's small ships, is all of 567 feet long. We took two helicopters and stuffed them, blades and tail folded, in an afterthought of a hangar above the missile deck.

These SH-60Bs had been built in the mid-1980s in the Sikorsky factory at Stratford, Connecticut. Silver metal plaques stating each helicopter's month and year of delivery, like birth certificates, were usually obscured by the copilot's boots in the cockpit. The two aircraft being retired on this day had deployed many times, on cruisers, frigates, and destroyers, with many pilots.

Before 1993, only men had the privilege to fly them. The helicopters that had hunted Soviet submarines during the Cold War or stood the watch in the waters off Kosovo were often nicknamed after pilots' wives or girlfriends. By 2011, the helicopters were just as often named for popular songs—my favorite was "Crazy Bitch," after the rock song—or reality TV celebrities. (The helicopter dubbed "Kim" was named for Kim Kardashian, although it wasn't meant as a flattering tribute.) I was among the last to fly the SH-60B. By the time of the official SH-60B Seahawk sundown ceremony in San Diego about two-and-a-half years later, all Navy helicopter squadrons had transitioned to the MH-60R, which boasted an all-glass digital cockpit, among other upgrades.

▲ ▲ ▲

We had flown from Florida to Arizona in a two-aircraft formation. It was my first flight over land in more than half a year, and I soaked up the green bayou vistas of the Deep South, grateful to be back in the States. After months of monochromatic shades of blue beneath the aircraft, a change in scenery was revitalizing. We refueled in landlocked cattle towns, where the concept of a seagoing service was as foreign as a Democrat. Our second-to-last day of our four-day, three-night "road" trip, we stopped in El Paso, just after sunset, and tied down the aircraft for the night, one leg short of our destination, after twelve hours of flying. We had been allowed three to five days to deliver the birds, with authority to deviate for weather or maintenance issues, as long as we kept our squadron apprised of our progress. Without saying it out loud, all four pilots seemed to want to delay the inevitable parting.

The isolated world of a warship at sea can be claustrophobic, and even the most serious of missions felt like a reprieve. We called it "air liberty"—flying low over the whitecaps, spotting dolphins in foreign waters, cloud surfing on lazy, quiet days in theater, and then the high-intensity night approaches to the rocking postage stamp of a flight deck. Our helicopters represented freedom, the way a teenager's first car does.

Over two deployments I logged nearly a thousand flight hours, and more than a year away from the States. My squadron changed in my absence, phasing in new helicopters that made the aging sweethearts I had taken to sea instantly obsolete. New pilots, fresh from training in the shiny MH-60R with its new-car smell, were my peers, sort of, but they made me feel like a dinosaur clinging to the steam gauges of the '80s.

The military has a lifecycle plan for every war machine purchased, and the original intended lifespan of a SH-60B was 10,000 hours. When a replacement helicopter wasn't quite ready, a paperwork drill extended the limit to 12,000 hours, then 13,000. The engineers at Naval Air Systems Command implemented a system called Fatigue Life Management, limiting flight time to eighty hours a month per aircraft, to offset extensions. The 60B, dubbed a "legacy" helicopter as new ones rolled off the assembly line, were all I'd known, and the boneyard delivery offered me a chance to say goodbye before shore duty. I would continue flying, in the MH-60R, at an operational test squadron, but it wasn't quite the same. Something about flying an aircraft with more flight hours than I had was reassuring, and I was grateful to the 60B for her early lessons.

▲ ▲ ▲

The boneyard workers handed Sharpies to the six aircrew from the two birds so we could sign the tails of the aircraft. I wrote my name and rank above the gray bird's bureau number, 163237, an aircraft's equivalent to a social security number. As I signed, I recalled all the hours I had spent in a 60B, learning what it meant to be a Navy helicopter pilot. The boneyard crew offered me a receipt after I signed a custody release form. Unsure of what to do with a receipt for a (slightly used) multi-million-dollar helicopter, I folded it and slipped it in the leg pocket of my flight suit.

I ran my hand across her rivets one last time, and walked away.

In Of Bees and Bumbling Men, *Nancy Brewka-Clark's*
protagonist remembers the events that led her to leave her
small-town Southern roots behind.

Of Bees and Bumbling Men
by Nancy Brewka-Clark

WHEN they first started talking about this writing project down at the
senior center, I thought they were all off their rockers. An article in the
paper claimed you could change your past by recalling painful things
and twisting them to your satisfaction until you told the story you wish
had been the truth. It was supposed to make you happy, but I couldn't
for the life of me see how. Why drag up things you'd worked hard all
your life to bury?

Then somebody said, once you put a memory down on paper,
it can't haunt you anymore. And somebody else said if you don't want
to poke around in the muck, and Lord knows at our age, we all have
muck that we may not want to poke around in, just write about the
good times before you forget you had any. My mama would approve
of that, I said, so I got me a six-pack of yellow, lined legal tablets and
a box of No. 2 pencils, and now I'm sitting here at the table in the

kitchenette conjuring up what Marvel Junction looked like back when Hector was a pup.

That's the kind of local expression my beloved Robbie would use, something he picked up from his granddaddy, Robert Munford Yarborough Beaufort, Jr. The old man always said he was from 'Carolina' because he just couldn't bear the feel of 'North' in his mouth. He had a surveyor's map older than Mason and Dixon framed on the front parlor wall. I always thought it was funny, how the line swerved to make Marvel Junction just south of where the border between the Carolinas would someday be. I suspect he drew that line in himself with brown ink from stewed acorns like the Cherokees used to cook up.

The old man passed away a long time ago now, but I didn't seem to recall it being all that long until I went into Gussie Grommet's antique shop here in Tallahassee. I tell you, it gave me a terrible shock to see that Ginny doll staring out of her pink box with the cellophane window. I had one just like her but she was taken away almost as soon as I held her in my arms. This one was immaculate, even the cellophane was in mint condition. When I tipped the box back, her eyes shut, and all I could think of was one of those poor little tots back in olden times who'd been mistaken for dead and prematurely laid to rest in lace and ribbons.

According to Robbie's granddaddy, wrongful burials happened so often they started making coffins with a window in the lid so they could rescue someone from being buried alive if they saw breath misting on the glass. Of course, all funerary rites occurred in the home then, mostly at the hands of the same women who delivered the babies. Bodies didn't get embalmed, and in the heat, they couldn't linger aboveground, so a person in a coma or in some terrible phase of paralysis could sometimes be washed and shrouded without anyone noticing they had life in them yet. Some folks even started getting buried with a long pole sticking up out of the coffin with a bell affixed, for fear they'd be buried alive up in the old Oak Grove Cemetery, and come to only to find themselves six feet under.

Oh, dear Lord, I don't want to be going there, not to Oak

Grove Cemetery. Truth to tell, most times I forget about that old burying ground altogether. But every so often my mind wanders and I find
myself going up through the tall weeds, shouldn't call them weeds,
since they were as pretty as anything in a garden, those bright red cardi-
nal flowers, and pink turtleheads, and the funny ones, those Turk's cap
lilies that turn themselves inside out like they're trying to heave their
guts up, listening to them swish most pleasantly as I pass through the
black iron gates and follow the old hearse path to my mama's grave.

It has never once crossed my mind in all these years to give a
plug nickel about where they put Daddy when his time finally came.
No, wherever his mortal remains lie, in a potter's field or prison yard, I
don't wish to be reminded of him nor how he murdered my beautiful
mama. Manslaughter, they called it, because his lawyer said of course
he didn't mean to kill her, it was just a spat that turned ugly. While
they'd always had words after Daddy'd been drinking, this time push
came to shove, and bang, my naked mama went over backward into the
white porcelain tub, where her skull cracked wide open.

The upshot of this single rash act was that I became as good
as an orphan in the time it took for her bath salts, rose scented, she
loved roses, to dissolve in her spilt blood. The only person I ever told
what it was like, coming in on her and seeing her eyes wide open staring up at my daddy while he howled to high heaven, was Robbie. He's
the one who gave me that Ginny doll, not Daddy, oh, no, my daddy
wasn't the type to be thinking of a little daughter's joy, now was he, or
he wouldn't have murdered her mama.

Robbie came to my eighth birthday party and he brought me
that Ginny doll as a present. This was way back in the middle of the
last century, mind you, when little boys didn't even attend little girls'
birthday parties, never mind give them a big box wrapped so prettily
with pink paper covered with deeper pink roses, with a big pink satin
bow on top, and a sweet little card almost as lacy as a Valentine, with a
painting of a little dog and a kitten snuggling in a basket.

"Two of a kind," my mama said, giving Robbie a big hug and
sending me a smile that had a message in it, like she thought Robbie

and I belonged together even then. He didn't have any brothers or sisters and neither did I. It was just him and his mama, his daddy having been killed over in Korea the very first month the war started back in June 1950. Robbie never roughhoused, preferring to sit and read, or to draw and paint with me. My mama attributed this artistic quality to his mama and her quilting bees.

Starting when I was a baby, Mama would walk over on Monday, Wednesday, and Friday mornings so I could play with Robbie and the other babies while the ladies worked on a quilt the size of a double bed on a frame that ate up most of the kitchen. This was in the early years after World War II, when everybody was infected with a fever to go back to a time when ladies had nothing more on their minds than whether their gloves matched their hats or what kind of aspic to serve. Since nobody had help anymore, the men writing ads for the magazines and radio and television showed more and more clever ways for a woman to cook and scrub. If there was any kind of thought put toward higher learning for their daughters, I never heard a soul mention it, just ways to brighten laundry.

When Mama died, Robbie came and put his head on my shoulder, resting it there to comfort us both.

My daddy murdered my mama two days after my party.

▲ ▲ ▲

I had to take a pause there to catch my breath. It still pains me to remember all that transpired after Sheriff Parker took Daddy away to the county jail, me wearing the same dress to Mama's funeral that I wore to my eighth birthday party, my hair all in a snarl because I kept twiddling it between my fingers to make tight little balls I tugged out by the roots.

It was an act of pure providence that Mama's sister couldn't make a go of it as an actress out in California even though she was the spitting image of Jayne Meadows, because she came back to Marvel Junction to care for me. First thing Aunt Betsy did was have that big old claw-foot tub wrenched out and a modern shower stall put in, bless her heart. The second was to install a TV, which drew Robbie like a magnet, especially the six o'clock news and the *Huntley-Brinkley Report,* where the two men talked about the world at large.

When we turned sixteen, Robbie started saying he'd go away to college in a place where nobody knew your granddaddy or ate boiled peanuts. I listened without complaint because when it actually came time, he would surely stay close by at Chapel Hill, and take me as his wife. He loved me and I loved him. I don't even know who said it first but it was always there, like the cat and the pecan tree and the cotton blossoms out in the old furrows bursting their heads wide open after Robbie's granddaddy passed and nobody coming to pick them, until they finally died away, too, and the tall grasses took over the way they did at Oak Grove.

In the March of our senior year, Robbie showed me his acceptance letter from an art school up in Boston, and said he was going. I made plans.

After the prom, we snuck back into his house and up into his room. His mama being a hard worker, was also a deep sleeper. Besides, I had no fear of her should we be caught because she loved us both. Once Robbie and I got beneath his quilt, a piece of fine handiwork stitched in the Jacob's Ladder pattern of black and blue diamonds on purple squares, I expected magic, fireworks, or at least the opportunity to keep him tied to me forever, even if it took a baby to do it.

He held me and stroked my hair and said how good it smelled and how good I smelled and he even kissed me on the lips, but then he just smiled and said I looked like I was hungry and did I want some of his mama's chess pie and sweet tea because he surely did. For some reason that made my heart ache and I commenced to cry until he promised, solemn as a judge, that he'd never look at another girl. And then he said that when he was up in Boston, he'd think of me every minute until he was home again for Christmas.

And, mercy on me, I believed him.

▲ ▲ ▲

Robbie showed up with Xavier during spring break. I was working at the Piggly Wiggly over to Tabor City, as a cashier. Robbie and I had never sought the companionship of others, which is why it was like a knife to the heart when he pulled up in his sweet little Volkswagen Bug, brand new from someplace up in Boston, because we still didn't much cotton to foreign cars in these parts back then, and there was Xavier looking out the side window like some kind of big, ugly dog. Why, if he'd nipped my hand, I wouldn't have been surprised. But I had to act happy, and so I did, for Robbie's sake, even though on the inside I was quaking from sheer, mortal terror.

What had I done, or what did I not do, for my best friend and lover to require a third party? That's what I wanted to know, but there wasn't any tactful way to ask. So, I just tagged along behind as we all walked up that old path to the graveyard, because Robbie wanted his new friend to see his great-granddaddy's memorial. It sat smack dab in the middle of Oak Lawn, a square granite base with an obelisk six feet high dedicated to Sgt. Robert Munford Yarborough Beaufort. He took a bullet to the heart at the Battle of Chickamauga while serving in the 58th North Carolina Regiment on September the 20th in the year of our Lord 1863.

An outsider couldn't decipher one weather-beaten word, but I knew it all by heart. When I started reciting the lines that Robbie's granddaddy so often declaimed, "Land of the South!—imperial land!—" Xavier turned to me with the most evil expression on his face.

"You lost," he said.

My eyes flashed to Robbie, wishing he had the sword of his ancestor to smite such hatefulness. "This poem isn't about that," he said. "The only reason it's on there is because Mr. Abraham Beaufort Meek, a relative on the Beaufort side, wrote it back in the 1840s or something. It's not even about the Civil War."

When he saw the expression on my face at the use of the Yankee name for our terrible conflict, Robbie gave me a smile that sent chills up and down my spine, so shallow and free of caring was it.

"That," I told him using a voice I'd never heard myself use

before, "is like something Traitor George would say."

His eyes opened wide, but before he could issue a comeback, Xavier said, "King George the Third?"

I looked him over the way one would a bad dress. "No, sir," I said, "General George Thomas, the Virginian who led the Army of Northern Aggression against this boy's great-granddaddy at Chickamauga. And what's a Mexican care about it anyway?"

As soon as I said it I didn't regret it for being the hurtful thing it was, but for casting a poor light on the manners of the girl that Robbie loved. While we were all awkwardly gawking at each other, very faintly, off in the distance a good deal away but not quite out of earshot, a bell commenced ringing, tiny peals jittering like an anxious hand had laid itself on a hotel desk bell.

"Do you hear that?" I asked Robbie, but he just kept looking at me, not sorrowfully, exactly, but the way I imagine my mama might have looked at me if she'd caught me smoking out behind the barn. "Think someone's coming back from the dead?" I asked, throwing a glance at Xavier so he'd ask what it was we were sharing and I could tell him: *nothing in this world.*

Robbie let out a sigh, then reached out his arms.

Xavier went into them as naturally as a ship sailing into port.

"No!" I remember the scream, and am quite certain it was mine because no one else there in that graveyard was denying anything, being alive, being dead, being loved, everyone in the ground and outside of it all knowing exactly who and what they were, except for me.

▲ ▲ ▲

One might think that such a trauma might have awakened me to the vagaries of the human heart, how to truly love someone is no guarantee that their love for you is commensurate with your own for them. But all I can say of that day is that somehow we managed to get ourselves out of that graveyard and back to his mama's house. By the time the two of them left for Myrtle Beach, I had already rewritten that scene in my own mind until it merely reflected the generosity of

Robbie's loving heart.

He never again brought Xavier or any other friend down to Marvel Junction, which made me as happy as it was possible to be, since I was always saying hello to him just to end up saying goodbye. I assumed that after he graduated he'd come home and find work in one of North Carolina's bigger cities, preferably not too far away. Robbie had another plan in mind, though, and enlisted in the U.S. Army. This actually surprised everyone else more than it did me, because I knew it was the Beaufort blood calling him to serve his nation.

We exchanged letters just about every day, but I didn't have to read between the lines to see his interests would never bring him back home. Oh, I hoped and prayed on it, but I pretty much knew we were fated to be sweethearts from afar when he called to say he'd gotten a fantastic job in San Francisco and I'd have to come out for a nice, long visit. Of course, I never did, because by that time I was manager of the Piggy Wiggly and I was preoccupied with that, and all the activities that still made Marvel Junction my heart's home then.

Robbie's been gone more than a quarter of a century now, taken in a scourge some said was biblical. You'd think I'd have worn a path to that old obelisk sticking up so hard and proud into the North Carolina sky, to visit him, but ashes and dust came to be too much for me to bear. So, I did what I never thought I could do, and moved away. But every night I go to sleep under Jacob's Ladder with my love for him as fresh and free as it was the day he gave me that baby-doll gazing out so lifelike from the box with the window on the lid.

A Guardrail

by Jack Mackey

If only I had fallen to earth
Hephaestus-like
on shattered legs
even one day earlier,
hobbled
I would have forged
my father's defense
of the strongest steel
before you walked that road.
Instead
today
I paint your name—
where drivers might notice
might slow briefly
might pause—
on this bent and rusted reminder
hammering my blazing brush
in brilliant colors
bellowing your name
into the gale.

John Guzlowski set out, in his words, to write about the glory and the shit he had in him. Raw and stark, our next story shows he succeeded.

1968: A True Confession
by John Z. Guzlowski

Part 1: The Siege of Khe Sanh

VIETNAM wasn't much in my life that spring.

Marching in the anti-war demonstrations, I wore a Vietcong hat made out of construction paper, but I wasn't thinking about war. My thoughts were all on love, the pure hippie girl yearning for me and the dreams we wove in the letters we were sure would bring us together finally in California after college.

I wanted to touch her, feel the weight and shape of her breasts as she rolled her gray sweater above her head and said, "Don't be so shy, Johnny. Don't you love them?"

And I did. I loved them more than our dreams of California beaches and waking in a house among green and red flowers with the scent of sunlit breezes stirring the curtains softly, softly but not enough to wake her from her dreams, just enough to wake me so I could follow the curve of her chin and imagine the taste of her hair in my mouth. Vanilla, sweet apricots, and something salty, maybe my sweat when we made love.

Those dreams kept me writing to her, but they weren't enough. So, while the soldiers in Vietnam pressed their backs against the sand-bag shacks of Khe Sanh, I told my parents that college was driving me crazy, and I dropped out and hitched 23 hours to College Park, Maryland.

But none of it worked out the way I imagined.

She was still in school, writing a paper on Crime and Punishment. She knew I loved that book, and asked me what I thought Raskolnikov's final sin was. Was it pride that drove him to drive his axe into the old woman's head, or was it the love he felt for his sister and mother? I couldn't think straight and made up stuff about Jesus and the Greeks and how hubris is a good man's failing.

And sometimes at night we'd walk the lazy, springtime paths of the campus, stop at a bench in the shadows, and neck and pet, or if we were lucky and her roommate was out, we'd sneak into her dorm room and press against each other, my hands on the breasts beneath her gray sweater, her palms rolling soft circles on my chest.

But mostly, she spent her time in the library, and I sat in an all-night diner dreaming and spinning a silver dollar on the counter.

Part II: Dreaming

Later that summer, we were in my parents' house, the rooms quiet with sunlight streaming through the windows, spinning the rooms to gold, and she said she didn't love me.

She said she had hitched from Maryland to tell me she was seeing me for the last time, that my love wasn't enough to keep her dreaming of California with me. She said she was moving to Frisco alone, and this was the end of us.

I went to my parents' bedroom and pulled a revolver from a drawer, and I didn't even know if the revolver was loaded or if I was just joking, and I grabbed her arm so tight she couldn't pull away, and

I pointed the revolver at her face and said I'd shoot her and then I'd shoot myself because she didn't love me.

She looked at my hand grabbing her arm so tight, and then she looked at the revolver and said, "If you're going to do it, do it—because I don't love you and don't I care if I go to California alone or die here with you."

And I said I'd do it. I'd take the revolver and pull the trigger. I couldn't live without us dreaming about California and cold beaches and red wine, all those dreams that filled our love with all the glory and beauty, all the time and sunlight, we'd ever need.

And she said, "Just do it. Just press the revolver there and do it."

And I knew I couldn't—not there in my mom's kitchen with the sunlight so pure almost like the sunlight on the cold beaches in California, and I let the revolver drop to the floor and told her I couldn't do it.

And she said it again, "I don't love you."

I couldn't look at her. I turned away and asked, "What do we do now?"

And she shook her arm loose from my hand.

Part III. Here/Now, 2015

What can you do after something like that?

We went out for coffee and talked, but there was nothing to say.

She moved to Frisco, and I finished my degree and started another. And all the while, I was writing her letters that didn't say anything because they couldn't, and she'd ignore them, and sometimes during spring break, I'd hitchhike to California.

I'd just stop by to see her. I wanted to see if she had changed, if the dream we shared had somehow pieced itself back together.

But it never did, and I met someone in grad school, and we got married, and got jobs, and bought a home, and loved each other like I never dreamed, and we were happy.

And sometimes I still think about the pure hippie girl and the weight and shape of her breasts as she rolled her gray sweater over her head, and I remember the taste of her hair in my mouth. Vanilla, sweet apricots, and something salty, maybe my sweat after we made love.

But it's different.

I'm sixty-six now, and soon I'll be sixty-seven, and what I've learned about life's changes is that we change the way the great glaciers change. Slowly.

One year we melt a little. The next we freeze a little. A wind comes from someplace and shines up our northern walls. The next year the wind is a little stronger or weaker. We don't change the way people in books change. Today's hero, tomorrow's fool.

Our future—a patient grandmother with a toddler in hand—comes slowly.

We explore another aspect of coping with death and survival with our next story, by Scot Friesen. Can we ever know what unwitting influence we may have on others?

Surviving Strangers
by Scot Friesen

Tᴏᴍ Davenport slipped an orchid lei around his neck and dug through the items jammed into the trunk of his car. He found a small bucket, which he filled with about an inch of paint, and stuck a tapered brush in his back pocket. He also grabbed an old canvas duffle bag he used to hold tools.

He was lucky the tall grass on the side of the freeway had been trimmed recently. The last few weeks had been a mix of rain followed by a few days of sun, and more rain. Even though this was typical weather for northeast Oregon this time of year, it made his work harder. The highway maintenance person had trimmed both shoulders, but left a three-foot circle of growth around the small, weathered cross. A few of the taller grass blades brushed the bottom edge of its arms. Tom searched the stained and faded bag of tools until he found the garden shears. He knelt in front of the memorial, and cut the fresh grass as close to the ground as he could. A careful stroking with a wired brush removed the peeling paint to expose the grey-bleached wood beneath.

"You're the one, aren't you?"

Tom lost his balance and fell onto his side trying to turn around to see who had snuck up behind him.

"Sorry to startle you, but good save on the paint," said the woman standing over him.

He didn't realize he had shifted his arm to keep the bucket upright. He set it on the ground, and rolled onto his back to look up at her. Sunlight glinted off the metal bits of her police uniform. "The one what?" A small drop of paint rolled across his thumbnail. The semi-gloss rolled to the edge of the nail, but there wasn't enough to go any farther.

"The guy that fixes up the roadside memorials."

The paint pooled on the edge of his nail like a cresting wave frozen in time, refusing to crash on the rocks. The woman's shadow slid across him as she leaned forward. She wiggled her fingers to capture his attention, and she helped him get to his feet.

"You've been on the news," she said. Her eyes traced the lei around his neck. Was she counting the flowers? He couldn't resist running his fingers over the purple dendrobium orchids. The petals were cold, wet silk against his skin. Dendrobiums had been one of his wife's favorites.

"I don't watch the news," he said, realizing she had shifted her gaze to his eyes.

"Need some help? I'm at the end of my shift."

Her nameplate said Adams and her uniform was spotless. Tom shook his head at her concerned look. "I'm okay, Officer Adams."

"You can just call me Laura," she said. Her brow furrowed a little.

"Tom," he said. "I'm okay, really."

"Nice flowers." She returned to her squad car, which was parked behind his Toyota, and waved at him before driving away.

The air around him seemed to empty as she disappeared around the bend. He had never been caught in the act until now, but he should have accepted her offer.

He took his time painting the cross to make certain the exposed wood and remaining old paint received a good coat. An empty potato chip bag, driven by the wind, bounced along the ground. He smashed it flat with the sole of his boot, and picked it up. A few crumbs poured out the open end when he shoved it into a garbage bag. He wandered the area, collecting trash, until the paint dried.

The purple lei woven around the arms of the cross stood out against the white paint.

▲ ▲ ▲

Three weeks later, Tom was standing in line at The Percolator Café. He hadn't frequented the coffee shop this late before, and he was surprised there were so many customers.

"Hi, Tom." A woman's voice called out behind him.

The past few days had been difficult, but he tried to smile as he turned. It was the police officer with the crisp uniform.

"So, you're famous now," she said.

For the first time in months, he tried hard to smile. "Good evening, Officer Adams. Laura," he said. "You didn't tell them about me, did you?"

"No way," she said.

"Thanks, but they found me anyway. I walked out my door a few days ago to twenty reporters camped out on my lawn."

"It was only a matter of time," she said.

"Later would have been better." He stepped away so she could order.

He took a seat in the corner with his coffee cup and watched the people come and go. Laura sat next to him, instead of opposite, with her back against wall. Her closeness opened a hole in his gut. He thought of his wife. They would sit in this very spot, always touching, either pressed lightly together or holding hands, as they sipped their beverages. Her closeness made him uncomfortable. He cradled his coffee cup in both hands because he didn't know what to do with his other hand. Laura spun her blended drink in small circles between short pulls on the straw.

"You're out late," she said, after they'd sat in silence for a few minutes. Her fingers left trails in the condensation on the plastic cup. Water beaded and slid down the sides to the table with each turn.

"Couldn't sleep."

"Coffee won't help that, you know."

"I know. I just wanted to get out of the house for a while."

"How's it going now that everyone in town knows who you are?" she asked.

"I avoid the reporters, but people from everywhere are sending me stuff. Yesterday I received a bunch of packages from some guy in Portland. He hand made ten crosses out of cedar. They're intricately carved, amazing work."

"That's nice," she said.

Tom fought the voice screaming in his head. You don't understand.

He shoved the table out of the way. Everyone in the shop watched him push his way through the door and almost knock a teenager down in his rush outside.

His eyes blurred with tears. The cool night air chilled the sweat building on his forehead, but it did nothing for the heat in his chest. His jacket insulated his burning skin, so he ripped it off, abandoning it on the pebbled concrete. He sat in a metal chair and wept into his hands.

Laura's voice sank past the ringing in his ears. "Tom… Tom… What's going on?"

She placed their cups on a black metal table nearby and dragged a chair closer to him. She sat directly in front of him this time.

"Please tell me," she said.

Tom shook his head. "You wouldn't understand. I can't do this anymore."

"My father died on the side of the road in a small town up

north."

"Did you go to the place where he died?"

"I did," she said, after a minute. A tear rolled down her cheek.

"Then you wouldn't understand," he said, hugging himself.

"Give me a try," she said. She stood and picked up his jacket from the ground, wrapped it around his shoulders, and sat back down. Tom pulled the jacket tighter around himself. Her eyes stayed on his. She never touched the tear. It dried and disappeared on its own. His tears were scars massing on his soul. He could feel the weight of them pulling him under.

Laura sat with her hands cupped in her lap. Their forgotten drinks cooled and melted at the same time, half finished.

"They died. My wife and my daughter. They died. My wife on the side of the road. My daughter a day later, in the hospital. I saw the accident on the news, but I didn't know it was them. The car was so mangled."

Laura leaned forward. She didn't say anything, but her eyes pressed him for more. More than he had told anyone. More than he wanted to tell.

"I wanted to go. I still try to go. Every day I get in my car to drive out to the site of the accident, but I can't because I'm scared." His voice was ragged, and his throat dry.

"Why, Tom?"

"I'm scared I won't say goodbye. I sit in my daughter's room every night and read Goodnight Moon to Snuggles, her favorite stuffed bear. That bedtime story was my wife's favorite when she was a kid, and now it's my daughter's. If I go out there, I may not come back." He couldn't stop crying.

"So, you drive up and down the freeway to care for the memorials of other people's loved ones," she said.

Tom nodded. "I never go near where it happened, because I'm a coward."

"People think you're a hero," Laura said.

He shook his head. Energy seeped from his body like water

squeezed from a sponge.

"You give people inspiration. You show them a stranger can do something nice. You keep the memory of their loved ones alive."

"I do it to hide from my own grief," he said.

"You do it to cope with your grief," she said. "I think I need to show you something."

Laura stood, and walked a couple of steps toward the parking lot.

"Come on," she said over her shoulder, not waiting for him.

Tom didn't want to get up, but he slipped into his jacket and followed her to her cruiser.

Silence filled the car as they drove, but he knew where she was taking him. His heart pounded. The hole in his stomach opened into a chasm.

The car made its way onto that stretch of highway he always avoided. The surface had recently been repaved. There were no pot-holes, no road noise. They floated along in the moonless night, sway-ing with the motion of the car. The lines hadn't been painted yet. An occasional reflector tab zipped by, glowing white before falling back into darkness.

Laura's face was washed with the light from the dash and computer.

"I don't think I can do this," he said aloud, but more to him-self.

"You're not alone. You must realize that."

Tom gripped his knees, fighting an incredible urge to leap out. He could feel the car slowing, and eventually rolling to a stop. He didn't realize he was clenching his eyes closed until he felt the car shift as Laura got out. The smells of damp grass and fragrant smoke drifted to his nose. His teeth and lips were clenched so tight his jaw hurt.

He stood and held onto his open car door, trembling. The headlights and spotlights were pointed at the biggest roadside memo-rial he had ever seen. The flashing blue and red lights cast their colors across the small grassy field, slowly rising away from the road.

Laura held his arm and guided him forward. A pink teddy bear was the first detail that captured his eye. He knelt in front of it, but could not bring himself to pick it up. Laura carefully removed the bear from the other things scattered around it and handed it to him. He cradled it in his arms like a baby. The plush fur was damp with dew.

"This isn't just for them," she said.

Tom took in the flowers, stuffed animals, toys, and candles. There was even a pink bicycle with colorful tassels, training wheels, and a big pink bow draping the seat. "What do you mean?" he asked.

"Look," Laura said, pointing with her lit flashlight.

On a chain-link fence, several feet from the back edge of the huge memorial was a big sign that said, 'Thank You.' The sign was surrounded by at least a hundred other signs of varying sizes.

"It's for you, too," she said.

Tom began to cry again. He nestled the teddy bear in a bed of flowers. He stood among the bouquets and candles. Their scents mixed with the moist, night air and filled his lungs with each breath.

"Can we go now?" he asked.

"Sure," Laura said.

On the ride back to The Percolator Café, Tom thought of his wife and daughter. His wife wouldn't have wanted all the fuss, but his daughter would have loved it. He imagined her moving from item to item wanting to smell, touch, and experience everything. The gratitude of the people of Victoria City was overwhelming, though it came at the highest cost possible.

Tom opened the car door, but turned back to Laura. "Can we go again tomorrow?"

"Yes," she said. "Meet here at nine?"

He watched her tail lights fade away again.

▲ ▲ ▲

This time he drove. It was Laura's day off, so she wasn't in her uniform. The uniform was part of who she was, but the jeans and gray pullover sweatshirt were there for function alone. Time slowed almost to a stop on the drive to the memorial. Tom was hyper-focused, as if on a perilous trip that took hours instead of minutes. He gripped the steering wheel so tight his knuckles were white and his hands were so cramped he had a hard time letting go once they arrived.

The memorial was larger than he had realized the night before, and he took in every detail. He and Laura started at the fence and read every message. Some were almost unreadable from the sun and rain. Others were laminated, on heavy paper, and in bold print and would last until they were taken down. There were even pictures of some of the memorials he had fixed up, thanking him for looking after the memory of a son, a father, a grandchild. Most of the flowers were roses and orchids of almost every color and variety. Many of the candles were still lit. They relighted any that had blown out overnight, and replaced some that were spent.

Many of the toys were worn. Tom imagined they had been beloved memories, hidden away in boxes from distant childhoods.

Tom pulled one of the hand-carved crosses from his trunk and dug a hole in the middle of the memorial for it.

"You're right," Laura said. "Amazing work." She ran her fingers over the smooth, painted wood. The post and arms were almost three inches thick. The cross would stand almost four feet tall once in the ground.

Laura found the pink teddy bear and placed it at the base. They pushed the flowers, candles, and toys around the cross until the offerings enveloped it like the ocean does an island.

Laura left his side. She had gone back to the car, and was leaning against the passenger-side door, watching him.

For the first time, he imagined life beyond the death of his family.

"I miss them," Tom said on the drive back.

"I know." Was all she said.

Wayside Shrine

by Pamela Ahlen

No one to explain how dark the night might have been or bright the day, the road's long black bruise—only a thrush fluting minor thirds under pine and interrupted fern. Beyond the hawkweed and roadside swale, beyond the brook's murmuration, two crude crosses wound the woods—strung from one an immense tire, strung from the tire a frazzle-face doll. And atop the other that jolt of red—the new toy truck, its torchweed glaze, the faint whiff of Valvoline.

how to sing a psalm
wayside trees and offerings
forget-me-nots

In this timely essay, Mary Silwance uses her abortive attempt to bring aid to the Water Protectors at Standing Rock as a springboard for a broader exploration of our responsibilities toward one another and toward the planet that sustains us.

Best Laid Plans

by Mary Silwance

Wᴇ were showered with well wishes.

For our personal needs, we were offered subzero sleeping bags, tents, a pocket stove, glove liners, a lantern, seasoned advice for camping in single digits, food and money for the long drive.

For the Water Protectors, a friend donated a bag of OTC meds, another dropped off comforters. We were handed cash. Still others were inspired to donate online.

Then, just before our departure, a friend stopped by with a stone and feather. Years ago, the speckled grey stone from San Carlos, Mexico, had become her sacred stone. This week, it asked to be taken to a new home, to be among other holy talismans at Standing Rock. The consecrated feather, from a Peruvian shaman, had participated in countless ceremonies. This week, it too asked to be taken to Standing Rock.

When we left at midnight, I placed the stone and feather on the dashboard, powerful totems to lead the way. Yet another friend met us off the highway at 3 AM in the blustery Iowa cold, and filled our car with thoughtful equipment for the wintering Water Protectors. We drove on.

Like anything you do that matters, you realize you aren't doing it alone or just for yourself. As others messaged encouragement and warnings, I realized I was a conduit, carrying the energy, hopes, and intentions of countless others. I felt buoyed by this.

Then it started to snow. Hard. We couldn't see. We slowed down. Still couldn't see. Checking the weather and road conditions we realized, at 6 AM, we couldn't continue. We decided to head home. The drive back was full of doubt. Should we have pushed on? Should we have hunkered down somewhere and waited for the blizzard to pass? Could we have extended our trip? Maybe driving would have been better in daylight?

A 12-hour roundtrip. I had wrestled my conscience about the emissions of this trip before leaving. It was painful to burn that much carbon for no good to come out of it, contradicting and undermining the cause we were going to support.

I felt distraught. We had planned so carefully, carved time away to make this weekend happen. A friend was staying with my daughters, another friend got them off to school; we had folks at Standing Rock waiting for us, a car-full of useful gear to deliver. The rock and feather had insisted on this journey. What would happen to the energy, hopes and intentions we had been entrusted with? I felt like I had failed; let people down.

...oft go awry

Later we would find out that vehicles had skittered off the highway and roads were closed. Even snowplows were discouraged.

Besides check the weather when you plan a trip, what could I learn from this aborted mission?

This journey certainly wasn't about my personal pilgrimage,

finally participating in something I'd been following for years. It wasn't just about delivering practical items for the winter either; another group would take them.

As we briefly white-knuckled through the storm, I thought about how climate change disrupts our best-laid plans. Granted a blizzard in the Dakotas is not unusual, and had been foreshadowed by the Farmer's Almanac. But it got me thinking about the 22 million people displaced by climate change since 2008. What happens to the hopes and intentions of these refugees? We take for granted the ability to execute our plans, even if they're delayed by circumstance. What happens when we simply cannot? It's really inconceivable, isn't it? Yet it is an increasing reality worldwide.

I also thought about the sacred stone and feather keen on going to Standing Rock. Perhaps they want to take part in their planet's restoration as well. For too long we humans have placed ourselves in dominion over Earth, subjugating the earth and its elements to satisfy our intentions. But it is further hubris to now assume humans are the only beings capable of caring about and for the earth. The planet and its elements are living sentient beings, perhaps invested in the restoration of their habitat in ways we can't understand.

For now, the stone and feather wait on my mantle. Their intentions halted, they still do powerful work. Each day they remind me we humans cannot save the planet on our own. As conduit of the intentions and hopes of others I was buoyed and weighted with responsibility, both humbled and honored. Maybe restoration happens when we become humbled enough and honored enough to realize we belong to the earth and its elements and the earth and its elements belong to us.

How then do we manifest such understanding in our lives?

Realist Flowers Sir Awake

by Catherine A. Lee

Compelling need to pay respects
is freakin' me when learning
selfsame night of deaths of
both my Negro poet mentors.
Independently my lovers made
the choice to live not with me
but against this stubborn beauty
blunt, real, uncomprehending
of reality as flowers at a wake.

1. Professor Johnston's Lessons

Here's an item for alumna news
at my alma mater
Montclair State:
"homeland security"
that year 1970 shot to kill 4 students
at another state school
disrupted all our classes on
the date English term papers due.
Instead Professor Johnston
insisted on a teach-in
at the student lounge
a lucky break for me
to turn in poem instead of paper
earn myself an A,
impressionable I.

That should have been the
end of it, end of junior year
going about my summer
business returning through Big Apple
from overnight at boyfriend's in Bayonne
Professor Johnston on the bus
I did not greet him—
shrank from nonroutine encounters
as was my habit then—
same stop for the college
the only one
fate forced that conversation
I learned he had my 411
          facts he must have made
          concerted effort to acquire
chitchat with my favorite prof
departed with a promise
to take me to a reading
in the City.
I accepted eagerly.

I still have the train-fare stubs
and other fragments of
that quite impactful trip
We drank at Dylan Thomas bar,
the White Horse in West Village
that reading turned supremely
private, virtually virginally tight
there in his loft
          Percy owned imprinting press,
          knew what it was for
my near compulsion to inhabit
urban playspace Grand and Center

developed from discovery of Afro-Saxon hip
encounter not soon again to be.
I, naive available confused young woman
dogged him whole of senior year.
My fantasy persisted
after graduation into masters classes
where with academic aptitude
I failed in politics.
Years later I started monthly women's paper,
set type with IBM Composer, Compugraphic.
I thought he'd be impressed
after all that time, I sent a note.
He was, enough to order a design for
his *Dasein* X (2,3,4) Triple Issue—
I have the contract signed and galley proofs.
Cover letter signed with love
denotes my comprehension of our literary society
was not entirely imaginary,
as thought and action underlay the missive
sent with orange business card he letterpressed
with his name, both locations and our numbers at the time.
He also begged a loan, downpayment's what he said
salon named "Studio Tangerine" would be.

Then another card arrived
bearing that name Tangerine and
another Lee, Lorraine, a dancer.
We argued to his ultimatum:
"never contact me again."
Yet maintained that telltale
minimum connection: unpaid debt.
Heartsore, savagely betrayed
I hobbled on to found and wail my own stuff

women's jazz production 13 years. My
Sojourner paper lasted 30, every month.

Google stalking in another century
I found him mentioned in a book,
Black Chant, and read in someone else's
honorific hand:
Percy Edward Johnston died March 20, 1993
a heart attack returning from rehearsal with his theater troupe.
So there. I never did.
His loss
still bothers me.

2. Jazz is Our Religion

Beyond the Blues, if you can find a copy,
anthology of black poetry, has a Johnston entry
turn to page before, it is Joans.
Hum another tune: how I met tedjoans

My lofted life had turned a page, still
read stuff with musicians now and then
and produced jazz concerts here and there
caught ted reading at a Boston bookstore
exhibitions that were rare, considering the fly guy
lived in Paris and somewhere Africa.
Coiner of the concept "Bird Lives" so they say
also trumpeter and raconteur with whom I dared
to riff my own flavor of *surréalité*
"Bebop Tourists in Bird's Yard."
What else to say, we hit it off.
At 1369 Club, squeezed between

the jam and Liebman/Beirach duo
ted headlined "jazz poetry event"
with me and Free Lance Wife Revue,
my band. Surreal for real!
he mailed me letters papered with drawings

Jazz is Our Religion, so he offered
teducation:

> *I'll make a deal with you   lose weight   fifty pounds and*
> > *more*
>
> *Then we'll get rich and then go all around this globe   and on my*
> *Sixtieth birthday   we could even get*
> *married   Now aint that a good reason to lose and lose and*
> > *continue to*
>
> *lose weight?????*
> *Awright already you must be erupting with hate for me*
> > *especially when I*
>
> *mention the*
> *taboo to you (and me too) marriage   and the nerve of me*
> > *saying only when*
>
> *I be   60*
> *But you must remember this   a kiss is still a kiss*
> > *and a sigh is just a*
>
> *sigh   and*
> *the hip world will always Casablanca Dooley Wilson piano*
> > *Bogart going down*
>
> *on Ingrid   As Time Goes By….*
> > *Darling, do not ever believe that I do not deeply*
> > > *DIG you. I DO*
> >
> > *thats what they say when people get married   but*
> > > *surrealist say*
> >
> > *Pie Glue!*
> > *(G. Corso's poem Marriage, read it)*

This time, executive refused to take direction
willed not to hear of such proposal

Next century same night of reminiscence tracking
I hear of ted's demise the year before,
days went by before they found him cold.
Details shock enough to follow up, reading
Corso's poem where tragicomic explanation
lies in open casket.
ted took another wife,
I never did lose weight. My loss.
the truth   ted lives!
awake   thank you.

This triptych of flash pieces by Hal Ackerman deals with the passing of loved ones, whether into another realm or another home. Together these pieces are both ode and elegy to familial love.

Mother Father Daughter
by Hal Ackerman

Yahrzeit

SHE is on the commode when I find her, head bent forward nearly to the floor, arms reaching for her walker in supplication. Exhausted. Naked. The outline of her spine like the bent balsa skeleton of a kite, strong, and so close to snapping. She is horrified for me to see that she has soiled herself. *Why didn't you let me go,* she wails, as though I am the one who has tethered her to the earth. Her arm reaches behind her for the roll of paper. Her arthritic hand is excruciatingly slow, like the earliest crude demonstrations of robotics. *The day has come,* she says. And she means the moment she has seen draw closer during the years of her increasing diminishment. The moment she has beckoned death to hasten. She has pleaded with him to choose her, sent gilt invitations, decked herself in finery, entreated him with all her seductive power. But again she is the wallflower, passed over for younger women taken down with kidney failure, heart failure, cancer, and foul play. She would jitterbug with the least accomplished dancer at the table, his collar frayed and dingy, dirt under his nails, unshaved and slovenly; throw her head back and let her scarf billow out behind her if he would only take her home.

Why didn't you let me go!

I find leverage under her sallow cheeks and raise her across my shoulders. She looks no heavier than ashes and dry straw, but she has swallowed the shame of gravity and I feel my back give way under the strain. I envision the paramedics rushing to the scene, discovering a sixty-year-old man splayed paralyzed across his mother's naked body, wondering what depravity they have stumbled onto. I soak a washcloth under the warm running water, clean her toadstool buttocks, pat her dry, find a fresh set of diaper pants on the adjacent shelf, place one bamboo leg into them, then the other, carry her across the threshold and set her down on her bed. Her blankets and sheets are folded precisely; broken unlit matches on the nightstand. Beside the memorial candle, the bottle of sleeping pills is open. Those she has not taken are spilled like carelessly planted seeds. She has been a widow forty-three years today. I ignite the wick, and light flickers across the translucent skin of her sleeping face.

▲ ▲ ▲

On his final walk through your apartment, your landlord noted the nail holes in the walls. He has seen the patio screen shredded by your cat, and the dark nebula in the carpet alongside your bed, stained from the blood that seeped all night from your chest where the iron tongue of your walker punctured your onion-thin skin.

When the Mexican boys came with their moving dollies, wheeled out your dining room table and mahogany dresser, that was the last of it. Your home exhaled its life as you had done, reverted to its natural state. Person into body. Some walls with shapes. Some light. Strangely smaller than the way you had first seen it, your eyes like a little girl's, painting it full of possibilities. Outside your door, someone had already scratched two dark lines through your name, as you had done to lost friends in your phone book. There is some defiance in the decision to cross out, and not to erase.

We have been here and gone. Not *We never were.*

▲ ▲ ▲

It is the time of morning when I called each day to see whether you were alive. Out of habit or morbid curiosity, I press the single quick call button. The phone rings twice and a mechanized voice informs me I have reached a number that no longer is in service. She suggests that I check the number again.

I'd like to propose a short trial period for death. A Customer Service questionnaire: Are you enjoying your death? Is it all you had hoped for? Is the pain gone? Are they all there talking over the backyard fences waiting for you? Is dad still forty-eight and in love with you? Have you left the bent, chalky desiccated chaff of your body behind? Are you the woman in your wedding gown smiling hopefully into the future? Are you dancing?

The screen on the cell phone asks:

Do you wish to delete "Mother?"

Press 1 to confirm.

Press 2 to cancel.

Father's Day

I am looking at my parents' wedding portrait. She is holding a garland of white lilies. The train of her gown is spread before her, rippling like an arctic whirlpool. She is slender and fine boned with a trace of Kathryn Hepburn. She is looking into the future like it is a dream of deep water that she has been led to and then left alone. Depending on which version of the story you believe, she is pregnant with me or she is not. My father stands to her right. Your focus would not be drawn to him in a group of other men. Honor and principles do not readily translate to film. Though he is not tall, there is an easy erectness in the way he stands. He wears a cutaway tuxedo in the picture and a formal tie. His right arm is relaxed at his side. He is looking into the future like he has heard an unfounded but troubling rumor. He would live twenty more years, to the ripe old age of forty-eight. Could he have known he had such a short time prepaid on the meter? That his expiration date had already been stamped? That his limited number of heartbeats had been allocated? Until the last one slammed the iron door shut behind it? A thud in the chest? The gasp? The clutch? The fall? The whitened sheet his face would become? Had he seen himself already? Crumpled on the floor of the department store among the holiday shoppers? Did someone try to revive him where he fell? I do not know. Did anyone dive on his chest? Cradle his heavy head in her hand and wail, oh God? Did a frozen circle gather around him, looking down in puzzlement? I do not know.

I have lived two decades longer than he. My doctor has told me I can eat a steak without fear of dying of premature heart disease. I ask him how can he be so sure. He tells me to look at my birth certificate. I will not die of *premature* anything.

So now I am free to look closely at my father's face in their wedding portrait. I have looked away from him for so long, frightened of sharing his delinquent manufacture. His face is kind. His smile is not so easily found as mine, which is more accessible. His had greater value. Never sown indiscriminately. Our name means we are farmers, men of the acres.

We are Ackermen.

Whenever I wonder if he knew me long enough or well enough to love me, I imagine that he was given a basket of years and told to divide them between himself and his children. He took just what he could hold in one hand, leaving nearly the full weight of it for us.

Alfalfa

Her room smells of alfalfa even though she has taken the rabbits. The stages of her life have settled into an archaeology of smells. The sweet dander of guinea pigs. Sour turtle bowls. Saddles redolent of horse piss and her own gamy adolescence. Weed. Incense. Her first boy. Her second boy. When a friend lied about her at school and everyone believed it. When she did not make ballet.

I would rather think of alfalfa. Of her uncle's farm in

Kentucky. Her small hand on the wheel of the tractor. Looking with intent across the unplowed field. Her hair, white as corn silk. Her voice all made of music. Her spirit an unhunted bird, gathering bits of shiny colored things it saw that it liked.

I don't want to think of the empty bedframe waiting for the moving boys to dismantle.

The mattress is already gone. Gone with Ani Difranco and the 3 AM phone calls and everything that was nailed or taped to the walls. She has left behind the dresser that she built herself, refusing help. It wobbles like an ancient parent you have to help to the bathroom. The wrong size screws protrude from the knobs. The drawers are emptied chrysalises splayed open like the tongues of exhausted oxen.

She calls to give me her new phone number. I write it down, thinking it is something I should already know. Something I should be teaching her. She will know things first now. If she gets cancer, it is she who will break the news to me. I tell her that without her instructive derision I go into the world unfit for public display. Hair unkempt. Wearing unmatched socks. Tufts of spiny filament sprouting from my earlobes. I threaten to wear slippers and a tattered bathrobe to the supermarket. But she is unmoved by pity to return. So, I describe the cream of cauliflower soup I have made for dinner. The clever substitutions to keep it non-dairy. The artichokes and roasted yams.

Dad, she says, I don't live there anymore.

Ah, I say.

And now it is she who fills in the silence:

Don't you want me to live in the world and be self-sufficient? Isn't that what this whole childhood nonsense was all about?

No, I argue. After a certain point, I am opposed to metamorphosis!

But even that is not true. I tell her yes. Yes to everything. Yes and yes. And of course, yes. Only just, you know, not yet.

Negative Metaphor: My Dead Daughter's Lipstick

by Jackie Davis Martin

It is not like the fuzzy chicks.
It is not like Diet Coke.
It is not like the beat-up chair torn by the cat.
It is not like a cat.
It is not like her sweaters, stored in bins.
It is not like the boots from Boscov's worn to New York or Paris.
It is not like the sidewalk in Wilmington.
It is not like the bottle of foundation.
It is not like a pink bathrobe.
It is not like a new computer.
It is not like a Toyota truck.
It is not like a hug or a kiss.
It is not like her thick waist.
It is not like her shiny bangs.
It is not like meeting at the airport.
It is not like Chanel perfume.
It is not like a museum.
Or not like a rose garden.
It is shaped like her bottom lip.

*Our closing piece is a richly-imagined science fiction story
by Karen Bovenmyer, who writes that she has tried "to
explore what hope we have when there is no hope, the choices
we can still make, and the courage and perseverance of the
oppressed."*

Like a Soul

by Karen Bovenmyer

Me and Momma went to see the pod in the hayloft just before sunrise—it spun out of the shadows ever so slow, sheen glittering in the pale light, all black and dotted with gold. The pod looked like a little jewel, something a rich man wore on his neck, but when I reached to take it down, Momma caught my arm and hugged me close. "Leave it. Butterfly gonna hatch out of it."

I didn't know what she meant, not then, because hatching wasn't ever a good thing. Not here. Not with the Clickers.

We moved quick when we came down, so the overseer wouldn't catch us. Everyone had to be outside the barn by sunrise. If somebody wasn't on time, or was maybe drunk or sick, they got whipped. If somebody went missing and the overseer thought they'd run off, their kin were whipped until they were found. Almost nobody took a chance like that.

The Clickers hung Jefferson from a tree when they thought his brother was gone—he was gone only two days—the Clickers killed Jefferson just to show everyone they could. Then they found his brother, anyhow. Lettie said he went for a piss in the night and fell down into the river and died—but Momma said maybe he jumped. Maybe he thought he could swim past the Clickers. But nobody ever got away. We were trapped, waiting like that butterfly inside that pod, maybe fixin' to hatch into something else. Anyway, both of them were dead for no reason at all. All the Clickers stomped up a big fit, snapping their saw-tooth jawbones, clacking their graspers together.

But they didn't eat no one, and nobody hatched. Not that time.

When Jefferson hung from that tree, the morning rays lit up a sheen in the sweat across his thick face. But there weren't no gold dots. And there weren't no jewel at all about Jefferson. Lettie said it's been goin' on a year or more since someone split open to show a Clicker inside—all white bones and graspers and grabbing arms, uncommon long—and time for it to happen soon. Clickers hide deep inside folks, and nobody knows until someone starts screaming and the Clicker splits on out and scares everyone. Then the big ones come take the new one away. Lettie said it doesn't matter. Someday, we all gonna hatch Clickers, because that's how they make young. That's what we're for.

Momma said that didn't have to be true, that we aren't all going to hatch into Clickers. She said so up in the hayloft when she saw that pod.

"Rudy, do you know what's in that pod?" We watched it together.

"Butterfly," I said, just like she told me. "He's gonna fly up out of here."

"That's right," she said. "Fly up, up and away. Like a soul."

"He's gonna die?" I knew souls were things that flew away from people when they died, God said so. Lettie said a soul and a Clicker can't live inside a person at the same time.

"Yeah. He's gonna die. But first, he'll fly up out of this pod and look over the whole wide world. He'll find a girl butterfly and make babies, and then he'll die, just like he ought to." Then she hugged me again and rubbed my arms.

But I thought about that. Jefferson had no business being hanged. Lettie said so, and she got a slap 'cause of her mouthin' off. But she only said what we were all thinking. If the overseer had just waited, the Clickers would'a only lost one man, not two.

"Why does he have to die?"

"'Cause that's what God made him for."

"Then why'd God make Clickers?"

She didn't answer, just hugged me to her again, so I thought maybe God wasn't the one who made them. "Nothing lasts forever, Rudy. Not you, not me, not the butterflies. Not even the Clickers. Everyone has to say goodbye sometime."

I nodded my head against her chest, hearing her heartbeat under my ear, feeling the drops of her tears tickle the back of my neck. But I didn't want to listen. I didn't want that butterfly to hatch and fly away and die.

That night, I walked in the dark and I stole that pod. I wanted it to stay black and beautiful and glittering. I wanted it to stay safe in my palm. So, I carried it around with me, in my pocket.

I had it with me through the long hours of working in the field. I hid it during bath time. I tucked it in my pocket when it was time for cookin' and eatin'. I even put it in my mouth once when the Clickers came and touched us all with their forearms, poking and rubbing; spending extra time on me, like they knew I was hiding something. It tasted like dried leaves. At bedtime, I held it close to my ear to see if I could hear that soul inside getting ready to fly away.

It was in my pocket the morning Momma was gone.

They looked for her everywhere. They tied my ankles to a stool in the middle of the yard. I felt so bad, my stomach hurt something awful. Every time a search party came back with no Momma, the overseer hit me real hard to make me scream, so if she was hiding, she'd come running.

I tried not to—but I screamed after all, and loud too—because the Clickers came and snapped and poked at me. But they didn't string me up, just left me tied there and hurting.

Lettie limped up and gave me some water when no one was looking, and gave me some bread, but she couldn't do more—and I couldn't eat it anyway—my guts feeling all upside down. I had to stay there tied to that stool 'til they found Momma.

At night, I cried. Then I found the little pod in my pocket and turned it over and over again, waiting, just like that butterfly, for sunrise.

In the morning, I held it up to the light and the sun shone right through it. I saw all that glossy black was thin as paper. Something started pushing the sides, like a flower blooming, coming out striped orange and black. A crumpled ball sort of fell, like a drop, its wings soaking wet like it was in the river. It clung to the pod in my hand and rocked there, the wings getting bigger, flatter, fanning themselves, while the sun got higher, brighter.

I heard a clack, clack, clack. I looked over to the edge of the woods and saw a big group of Clickers coming, carrying something black that glistened in the light. It was Momma, and she was all wet. She was all limp and her eyes were staring. She wasn't split open, and there was no Clicker wiggling out of her. She didn't move at all.

I looked back down to the butterfly in my hand. I didn't want to look at Momma. The wings were full flat fans, now.

Lettie came over to me with tears washing her face, and the overseer took off his hat and nodded his head. Someone untied me from the stool.

I looked at the butterfly. It fanned its wings and took off, flying up, up over my head and above the barn. Like a soul.

And something deep inside me cracked open.

About This Book

The typeface in this book is 11 point Garamond with Gill Sans headings. The title on the cover is set in a variation of Handwriting Dakota. Funky typesetting reflects the requests of the authors.

Editor Susannah Carlson is a writer of short stories and poetry, and editor of whatever words happen to be in front of her at a given time. She has worked as a content and line editor for over two decades, and has seen a number of novels from rough draft to launch party. Susannah lives in Silicon Valley, where she was born, in a time when orchards still outnumbered office parks. She remembers feeding horses over her back fence just down the street from Hewlett Packard. Morbid by nature, she has always been drawn to roadside memorials, and it was her quest to discover the official term for them that led to the making of this book. Susannah's work has appeared in numerous journals over the decades, most recently, *Reed, Narrative,* and *Cahoodaloodaling.*

Descansos Poetry Editor, Wulf Losee, lives and works in the San Francisco Bay Area. He writes a poem every now and then, depending on the charity of his Muse—whose creative rationing system he doesn't fully understand.

About Darkhouse Books

Darkhouse Books is a publisher of mystery, science fiction, as well as literary prose and poetry via our *RIFF* series. We are located in Niles, California, an inadvertently-preserved, 120 year one-sided, railtown, forty miles from San Francisco. Further information may be obtained by visiting our website at www.darkhousebooks.com.

Authors' Notes

Hal Ackerman *Mother Father Daughter*

"The pieces were written at different times. *Alfalfa* was written the night after my daughter, then eighteen, got her own place, and where I lived was no longer home. *Yahrtzeit* was written the night after my mother died. Father's Day on an anniversary of my father's death."

Mr. Ackerman, former co-chair of the UCLA Screenwriting Program, is author of two mystery novels, an award-winning one-man play, and a recent collection of short stories titled, *The Boy Who Had A Peach Tree Growing Out Of His Head...and Other Natural Phenomena*. This piece was previously published in *I Wanna be Sedated*, and *Alfalfa* was published as a stand-alone in *Jewish Currents*.

Pamela Ahlen *Wayside Shrine*

"Last summer I attended the Breadloaf Orion Environmental Conference and had the fine opportunity to work with Aimee Nezuhukumatathil. One of our generative assignments was to explore the Breadloaf campus and surroundings, and write a *haibun* based on our findings. West on Vermont State Highway 125, I discovered the wayside shrine."

Pamela Ahlen is currently program coordinator for Bookstock Literary Festival In Woodstock, Vermont. She organizes literary events for Osher (Lifelong Education at Dartmouth) and has recently compiled and edited the *Anthology of Poets and Writers: Celebrating Twenty-Five Years at Dartmouth*. Pam is the author of the chapbook *Gather Every Little Thing* (Finishing Line Press).

Jon Black *So Lonesome I Could Die*

"Blending a classic ghost story with Texas Gothic, So Lonesome I Could Die, draws deeply on my background in music history, set against the backdrop of America's popular-music scene of the 1930s. The idea is one I'd been kicking around in my head for a long time, but could never really bring together. The *Descansos* angle serendipitously provided the piece the story needed to make it work."

Mr. Black is a freelance writer and journalist based in Austin, Texas, where he primarily writes about music, musicians, and music history. His first novel, *Bel Nemeton*, will be released this year.

Nick Bouchard *The Tall Man*

"*The Tall Man* is the product of an actual event (and maybe a little make believe). I saw the unfortunate rabbit from the first scene on my way to work. I wanted someone to put him out of his misery and give him a proper burial. Eventually someone did show up, just not as friendly a someone as I had hoped."

Mr. Bouchard is a father, husband, and writer. He likes baseball, old cars, and typewriters.

Karen Bovenmyer *Like a Soul*

"The monarch butterfly is a symbol of metamorphosis and rebirth for me. Often, I discover a story as I'm writing it, and that was the case here—I knew I wanted a little girl in dire circumstances to bond with and carry around a monarch pupa, and I wanted to link what was happening to the butterfly to the girl. I wanted the Clickers to act more like farmers and

163

merchants than horrors. I grew up on a farm and used that as the setting, finding myself in Rudy and Rudy in myself."

Ms. Bovemyer is the 2016 recipient of the Horror Writers Association Mary Wollstonecraft Shelley Scholarship. Her poems, short stories, and novellas appear in more than 40 publications, and her first novel, *Swift for the Sun,* was published this year by Dreamspinner Press. This piece has been previously published in Stonecoast Review (2013,) Creepy Campfire Quarterly (2017,) and 100 Voices Anthology (2016).

Nancy Brewka-Clark *Of Bees and Bumbling Men*

"My first professional writing job was as a full-time feature writer for a chain of dailies on Boston's North Shore. My editor hailed from a tiny town on the border between North and South Carolina. He was a complete gentleman, witty, handsome, single, and spoke in a luscious deep drawl. He was also alcoholic and gay, but this was 1971, so an astonishing number of people didn't recognize either characteristic. Although I was engaged and he had a girlfriend, we became inseparable. When he got a job on a better-paying newspaper, he brought me along. Eventually, he went to the West Coast, lost several jobs, and became a night motel clerk. The downward spiral finally brought him home, where he died."

Ms. Brewka-Clark's plays have been produced across the country and abroad. This year, her work has appeared or is forthcoming in *Routledge's One-Minute Plays,* the poetry anthology *Two Countries* by Red Hen Press, and a fairytale romance called *Musical Hearts* published by Less Than Three Press.

Diana Brown *Tatort*

"*Tatort* is a story of loss, and of a memorial that represents more than its inscriptions show. But it's also a story of shared suffering that creates bonds where they didn't previously exist. It's a reminder that when we are most alone, we are most a part of humanity."

In addition to writing, Ms. Brown is an IT professional in the Pacific Northwest. She spends her free time writing, and exploring her home state with her husband and dogs.

C.A. Cole *New Mexico State Highway 76*

Ms. Cole lives in Colorado and makes frequent visits to New Mexico. This piece was previously published in *Moonsick Magazine* (2015).

Teressa Rose Ezell *Tin-Tree Descanso*

"I have always been intrigued by roadside memorials. These reminders of unexpected loss never fail to elicit a moment of sympathy for the bereaved parent, partner, or friend. The title, "Tin-Tree Descanso," came to me first, and when I sat down to write the original draft, I allowed the story to unfold in much the same way that I sometimes "channel" a work of fiction. The poem's setting represents any number of roads and crossroads I have explored throughout the years. The bereaved and the person memorialized embody the many creative, fiercely independent free-spirits I have been blessed to know—those remaining, and those mourned."

Teressa Rose Ezell's poetry, fiction, and creative nonfiction have appeared in a variety of publications, including *The Magnolia Review, 99 Pine Street Literary Journal, Mulberry Fork Review, Apeiron Review, Bethlehem Writers Roundtable,* and *Main Street Rag's Coming Off the Line* anthology. Her environmental and political writing has appeared in *Countercurrents, ZNet,* and other national and international outlets. She earned an MA in English and Writing from Western New Mexico University and an MFA in Creative Writing from Lindenwood

University. She currently lives in St. Louis, Missouri. Connect with Teressa at teressa.rose.ezell@gmail.com, or via Facebook.

Ivan Faute *Watermelon Baby*

"This piece came from two places. The first was driving from Illinois through Missouri toward Arkansas and seeing cotton fields interspersed with watermelon vines. Along those back roads are old cotton gins, storage barns, and dozens of wagons, tractors, and trucks that tell a story through their abandonment. Only rarely did we see a shadowy figure, nevertheless the empty landscape showed the traces of productivity—past and present. The story also comes from musing about how loss and hope can occur simultaneously. Even as we are swallowed up in great sorrow, we can think about the future, the next thing, and how to make the world a better place for those who come after."

Mr. Faute's prose has been published in a variety of literary journals, and his plays have been presented in New York, London, and Chicago. He teaches creative writing at Christopher Newport University in Southeast Virginia. This piece was previously published in *The Mochila Review* (2008).

D. Dina Friedman *Flying*

"Flying stems from a real-life experience. I wrote the first draft many years ago, and actually read it at the funeral of the father mentioned in the story. Over the years I've revised the piece quite a bit, letting it cross that delicious border between fact and fiction so it can more fully and quickly get to the heart of what matters."

In addition to two young adult novels, Ms. Friedman has published widely in literary journals and received two Pushcart Prize nominations. She teaches at the University of Massachusetts, Amherst.

Scot Friesen *Surviving Strangers*

"I've had an odd fascination with death the last several years. I should clarify that statement before I start getting calls. I'm not interested in the morbid details, but the perception we have on death, the grieving process, and how we survive those who have left us behind. Our experiences and decisions write our final chapter in life. Our fear, suffering, sacrifice, cowardice, heroic, hateful, or loving reactions to existence shape how others see us to the end. *Surviving Strangers* is my latest walk down this path. The idea for this story came to me rather quickly while driving home one evening after I found out about the *Descansos* anthology. I've also been working on my first novel, so I couldn't resist adding one of its characters, Laura, as an anchor for Tom, even though she is still struggling with her own grief and loss."

A US Army veteran, Mr. Friesen's vocation is managing computers. His avocations are writing, photography, and woodworking. He lives with his wife in San Jose, California, the city in which he was born.

John Z. Guzlowski *1968: A True Confession*

"I've been writing since I was a kid, 60 years ago, but I only started writing about myself recently. When I sat down to write about myself, I promised that I would tell the truth about who I was. I would tell people stuff that I had never told my friends, never told my wife, never told my parents. I would write about the glory I had in me and I would write about the shit that was in me. The story True Confessions came out of that promise."

Mr. Guzlowski's writing appears in *Garrison Keillor's Writer's Almanac, The North*

American Review, and many other journals here and abroad. His poems and personal essays about his parents' experiences as slave laborers in Nazi Germany, and his life as a refugee in America, appear in his award-winning memoir, *Echoes of Tattered Tongues* from Aquila Polonica Press. This piece was previously published in *Flash Fiction Online* (2015).

Amber Colleen Hart *After Your Husband Dies – An Instruction Manual*

"*After Your Husband Dies—An Instruction Manual,* was inspired when, while watching my husband mow the lawn, I realized, if he died, I'd be forced to figure out how to use the riding lawn mower. It's a downward spiral from there, with a hint of hope."

Ms. Hart lives in Tennessee with her husband, children, and two maladjusted dachshunds. Her debut short story collection, *No Landscape Lasts Forever* (2016,) was published by Excalibur Press.

Terresa Cooper Haskew *Living the Dream*

"I participated in a fiction workshop and all participants were offered the same writing prompt, which was pretty much the first paragraph of my story."

Terresa lives in the Midlands of South Carolina, where she writes short stories and poetry. The winner of multiple writing awards, her work has appeared in numerous literary journals, as well as a collection of her poetry, *Breaking Commandments.* This piece was previously published in *Altered States* (*Main Street Rag,* 2011), and served as the inspiration for a short film.

Dave Holt *Desesperanza*

"The poem is based on a conversation I had with a customer in Arizona while I was working for Wells Fargo. I also visited friends on the Navajo reservation (in AZ) and saw their family hogan which wasn't being lived in anymore but my friend had stories of growing up in it. Drinking and driving is the third leading cause of death for Indians."

Dave Holt, born in Toronto, Canada, of Irish/English and Ojibway Indian ancestry, moved to California as a songwriter. He graduated from San Francisco State's Creative Writing program (M.A.), published in several literary journals, was featured in the Berkeley Poetry Festival, and has won several poetry prizes including a Literary/Cultural Arts award for his book *Voyages to Ancestral Islands.*

Terence Kuch *Thebes—The Coming of War*

"It was years ago that ancient and modern Greece suddenly collided for me: Trucks speeding their way to Colonus on roads where blind Oedipus once groped onward; radio towers shouting the latest oracle; thetes crowding into the Moschatou station between the long gone Long Walls.

"It was all there, all at once – all that time: the air the earth the sea the stones; what Sophocles told us about a place comfortably far from town; what Pausanias that wonderful tourist saw and half-believed; what Byzantines and Turks, Romans and Roma, and many others saw in this brown place: that the old gods may have abandoned Antony but never, quite, abandoned Greece."

Terence Kuch's prose and poetry has been published in the USA, Canada, UK, Australia, France, and elsewhere. A satirical poem of his won a New York magazine prize, was praised and reprinted in the *New York Times,* and included in a Random House collection. He lives in Springfield, Virginia, with a wife and several opinionated cats. Readers are invited to visit www.amazon.com/author/terencekuch .

Lita Kurth *Descanso for November 2016*
"In the wake of the election, I was so traumatized; everything around me seemed to hold metaphor. I couldn't read a book about ocean life without seeing it as a metaphor for our situation as a country. When the call came out for descansos, memorials, I immediately remembered the loss I felt when the Bernie hope died, and my mixed feelings about what was left. Of course, the resistance that is now alive and cooking makes me feel that good will still come of this disaster, so now I wouldn't say 'what we can't have again.' It's just that we'll have to work so hard just to get back to square one."

Lita Kurth (MFA Pacific Lutheran -Rainier Writers Workshop) has published in three genres and is a co-founder of San Jose's Flash Fiction Forum. She teaches and writes, publicly and privately and contributes to *TikkunDaily* and *Classism.org*. LitaKurth.Weebly.com

Catherine A. Lee *Realist Flowers Sir Awake*
Catherine A. Lee began exploring poetry as a percussive voice with jazz musicians at a loft she founded in Boston. From San Antonio, Cat explains the genesis of her self-explanatory poem: "Since teenage, I've hated pop music lyrics. I substituted listening to instruments, improvised jazz. That fluency made me stand out in a certain college English class, where a self-published, NYC-loft-living Afro-Saxon poet taught me something missing from my white suburban upbringing: artistic self-sufficiency instead of wage slavery. From linguistics graduate studies I jumped to my first job: a secretary using rudimentary IBM typesetting equipment. I kept up with technology (phototypesetters, then desktop publishing workstations) to create feminist periodicals. At a loft in Boston, I did the producing I observed being done in NYC by the professor. Later I met the griot, wowed him with familiarly surreal words/deeds. Decades later, doing in-depth research (in *Black Chant* by Aldon Nielsen), I was inspired to use 21st century keyword searches to Google-stalk my old flames. I discovered they were gone. So I've paid my dues, have the blues. To explore our inseparable stories, I wrote this poem to pair with spirit-filled music that literally heals skin-supremacist hate. That's why I make it."

Ellaraine Lockie *The Best Revenge*
"Our own 9/11 tragedy took on a dream-like quality because I was working in South Africa at the time. Seeing it on television without much coverage was like watching a surreal movie. The full effect of terrorism didn't register until I visited London soon after the bombings in their public transport system. Upon my arrival, I became immobilized by fear. I couldn't take a bus to my hotel, so I dragged my luggage and walked. I came to a sidewalk memorial for one of the girls who had been killed. The ability of the British people to rise above fear and so stoically get back on the Tube enabled me to do the same. "

Ellaraine Lockie is a widely published and awarded poet, non-fiction book author and essayist. Her thirteenth chapbook, *Tripping with the Top Down,* was just released from FootHills Publishing. Earlier collections have won the Encircle Publication Chapbook Competition, Poetry Forum's Chapbook Contest Prize, San Gabriel Valley Poetry Festival Chapbook Contest, Best Individual Collection Award from *Purple Patch* magazine in England, Encircle Publications Chapbook Competition and the Aurorean's Chapbook Choice Award. Ellaraine teaches poetry workshops and serves as Poetry Editor for the lifestyles magazine, *Lilipoh.*

Jack Mackey *A Guardrail*

This poem was inspired by the death of his fourteen-year-old son, Kevin. Jack Mackey lives in Rehoboth Beach, Delaware.

Jackie Davis Martin *Negative Metaphor: My Dead Daughter's Lipstick*

"I wrote "Negative Metaphor" in response to a prompt from Southeast Writing Regimen that instructed the writer to take an object of some value to the writer and present that value in opposite metaphors.

"I'd written a great deal about losing my daughter, but something I hadn't addressed was the way her lipstick had been worn into her lip-shape. I had gathered her makeup, irrelevantly, and had been haunted by that living example of something she had used. I found some satisfaction in presenting this account of all that I'd lost."

Jackie Davis Martin's recent stories appeared and won awards in *Flash, Flashquake, Enhance, Counterexample Poetics, Fractured West, Bluestem, On the Premises,* and *New Millennium Writings.* Her stories are included in several recent anthologies: *A memoir, Surviving Susan,* was published in 2012. She teaches at City College of San Francisco.

Cate McGowan *I'll Go Now*

"I aspire to poetry. I grew up reading Yeats, Keats, Frost. These were my bedtime storytellers. So, when I write prose, I echo the language I hear in my head and fall into a sometimes over-lyrical trap. I have to keep this propensity in check. I'll Go Now sprouted from the epistolary sections—they were originally stanzas in a long poem I wrote to my father. Indeed, poetry shapes my intellectual life, but trying to make sense of the guilt and confusion I felt after my father's loss constitutes the shaping of my emotional life. I wrote this essay for Father's Day last year, and it's helped me come to terms with Dad's passing."

Cate McGowan's fiction and poetry have appeared in *Norton's Flash Fiction International, Glimmer Train,* and *Crab Orchard Review.* Her award-winning collection of short stories, *True Places Never Are,* was published in 2015.

Brian Morgan *A Song for the King*

"I've learned through a series of growthful, often painful, experiences that failed relationships, or career opportunities, can generally speaking be drawn to a blind spot in my own armor, some place I think I'm defended when I'm actually vulnerable. Jason was an extraordinary talent, and I didn't, ultimately, know how to manage his excellence. Now, I simply revere it. I didn't publish this piece for years. This seemed like the right place."

Mr. Morgan is both a practitioner and teacher of writing, including his work as a member of the PEN Prison Writing Committee. His work has been featured in *Manhattan Magazine* and *Revolutionary John.*

Armine Mortimer *Thirteen*

"Thirteen grew from a glimmer of an idea: write a narrative in the future tense. To this was quickly added another constraint, which seemed odd even to me: make the narrative aware of itself as a story—a self-reflexive narrative. And quickly thereupon followed the knowledge that something dreadful was going to have to happen and the story would have to make sense of it.

"As an age, thirteen is one of the most delicate. The new teenager is fragile, prey to multiple definitions of self; if care is not taken, something can go wrong, without warning.

I wanted my young man to suffer that unbidden fate. The story could bring him to no other conclusion than that broken bow."

Armine Mortimer's work as a literary translator has been published in *3:AM Magazine*, *The Brooklyn Rail*, *AGNI*, and other reviews. She is also the translator of two books by Philippe Sollers: *Mysterious Mozart* and *Casanova the Irresistible*. This story is her first published fiction.

Kurt Newton *Angels of Mercy, Angels of Grief*

"As a horror writer, death is familiar territory. I've always been fascinated by the ritual of roadside memorials, and one day decided to explore that fascination in the form of a story. Everyone, at some point in their life, is touched by death. Most of us are wounded by it. Some are even haunted by it. A few of us become obsessed with it. The main character in *Angels of Mercy, Angels of Grief* experiences all three."

A writer of horror fiction, Mr. Newton's work has appeared *Weird Tales*, *Dark Discoveries*, and *Space and Time*. This piece was previously published in *Dark Demons* (2002).

Jonathan Ochoco *Waiting by the Window*

"I was having a drink with a friend at Moby Dick's, in San Francisco, and I mentioned that I had never been to Twin Peaks before. So, we went there for one more, walking past the bronze plaques on the sidewalk, which commemorate the lives of influential members of the LGBT community. I remember just how different a bar Twin Peaks was. There's a reason it's been nicknamed the Glass Coffin—because of its windows and older clientele. We sat by the window, and I struck up a conversation with a man at the next table, who was there with a drink, waiting for his husband of twenty years. Our conversation served as the inspiration for this story."

Mr. Ochoco came to live in San Francisco by way of Texas. A lawyer by training, he has recently returned to writing. More of his work can be found in *Fiction War* and *Gathering Storm*. Jonathan is also an avid curler and plays in a league in the San Francisco Bay Area.

Richard King Perkins II *Monuments of Absence*

Richard King Perkins II is a state-sponsored advocate for residents in long-term care facilities. He lives in Crystal Lake, IL, with his wife Vickie and daughter Sage. He is a three-time Pushcart, Best of the Net and Best of the Web nominee whose work has appeared in more than a thousand publications.

Frank Russo *The Road to Paihia*

"*The Road to Paihia* was written following a road trip through New Zealand's North Island several years ago. One of the features of the landscape that struck me was the frequency of white crosses beside the highways. In some places they appeared every half mile, sometimes in clusters, all of them displaying the same uniformity of size and style. I was intrigued and unsettled by this uniformity. After some research I discovered that the size, shape, color and placement of these crosses were all governed by strict regulations—any memorials which didn't conform to these regulations were removed. The poem was a response to the arresting scenery and the hundreds of white crosses that acted as a reminder of the high death toll on those roads."

Frank Russo is a writer of fiction and poetry based in Sydney, Australia. His poetry collection *In the Museum of Creation* was published by Five Islands Press (2015). His writing has appeared in various journals and anthologies in Australia and North America.

Nicole Scherer *Last Flight Out*

Ms. Scherer is a freelance writer and active duty U.S. Navy helicopter pilot, currently stationed in Yokosuka, Japan. She has a history degree from Marquette University, and a Masters in Science Writing from Johns Hopkins. From *Air & Space/Smithsonian Magazine* (November 2016).

Jesse Sensibar *Shrine Stories*

"I do a lot of wandering on the ghost roads of the Southwest, exploring both the landscapes and my own damaged past. Along the way I have many touchstones. The most frequent of these are the shrines I find along the highway. I have a deep connection to them as unique handmade spaces that are both sacred and profane. I document them as I find them with a photo and a short description including the location and often a bit of commentary on both the shrine and my own journey at that moment where the two intersect."

Jesse Sensibar works, wanders, and writes his way into and out of the high deserts and border towns of his disappearing American West. Jesse Sensibar loves small furry animals and assault rifles with equal abandon, and has a soft spot in his heart for innocent strippers and jaded children. His work has appeared in *Corner Club Press, Grey Sparrow, Journal, Niche, 4ink7,* and *Stoneboat Journal.* Jesse received the Reader's Choice Award for his fiction published in *The Tishman Review,* and his flash fiction was shortlisted for Pulp Literature Press's *The Hummingbird Prize for Flash Fiction.*

Mary Silwance *Best Laid Plans*

"*Best Laid Plans* is the manifestation of an intention, unrealized, to go to Standing Rock in November 2016. In fall 2016, some friends and I started the group One Less Pipeline to help raise awareness of the connection between our petroleum consumption to pipeline construction as an environmental justice issue. I had spent weeks deciding (didn't want to consume more petrol), then planning, then collecting gear and finally setting out. Seemed after all that I was supposed to learn something, and writing is what gets me to a deeper understanding."

Mary Silwance is an environmental educator and activist, farm hand and cofounder of www.facebook.com/*OneLessPipeline/*, poet, gardener, mother of three, and blogs intermittently on the intersection of spirituality and sustainability at http://tonicwild.blogspot.com/.

Tyson West *Foota Forever*

"In a part of our city known as Felony Flats, I came across a descanso in an alley for a teenager who had died there in a gang incident, which inspired this story. Although we do not have a lot of gang violence here, occasional descansos are set up for people who die in accidents. When an older Native American gentleman died as his prized El Camino fell on him while he worked on it, Code Enforcement forced his son to remove his descanso after a few weeks. As a landlord, I understand people are caught between the city's desire for order and natural human grieving."

Mr. West lives in the wilds of Eastern Washington State, where he writes poetry and prose, finding inspiration in his real-world employment in real estate.

Kevin Wetmore *Burial at Fishkill Creek off I-84*

"*Burial at Fishkill off I-84* is in some small ways autobiographical, in as much as I would drive from Pittsburgh, where I was in grad school, to visit my family in Connecticut. I have driven the route described in the story more times than I can count. I was also inspired by the end of a relationship to think about how we mourn such things and how we "move on." I also began to think about how one can drive the same highway with some frequency until the route grows as familiar as one's own home, and yet we know nothing about the places we drive through."

Mr. Wetmore's stories have appeared in numerous publications, including *Midian Unmade, Moonshadows, Restless, Mothership Zeta,* and *Weirdbook.* Despite being a Connecticut Yankee, born and bred, Mr. Wetmore now resides in Los Angeles, California.

Woody Woodger *My Blood Splatter Analysis of an Alcoholic's Excuse*

"This piece began as a piece of New Sincerity—dense, choppy lines, a speaker's sloshy malaise—and none of it worked. By the 4th draft, it had not distinguished itself from many other pieces in my a manuscript concerning my uncle's alcoholism. Before the 4th revision, it was relegated to the back as filler, a stale brick of styrofoam. The ending, however, was worth salvaging. I thought to experiment as my manuscript needed more experimentation and I thought it might be interesting to experiment with voice. I don't remember what inspired blood splatter analysis. Perhaps I was feeling Dexterish, but I Googled "blood splatter analysis handbook" and began extracting and supplanting the terminology I found. Through the language of crime scene, the poem became a tour of my uncle's house—a visual miasma of lies, small slights, drunken temper, and familial masochism. As a blood splatter report, the tone became clinical and the speaker's emotional inaccessibility heightens the tragedy."

Woody Woodger is a New England poet whose first chapbook, *postcards from glasshouse drive,* is currently forthcoming from Finishing Line Press. His other works have perviously appeared in *Barely South, Soundings East,* and *(b)OINK,* among others.

Fred Zackel *When You Least Expect it, a Jackrabbit*

"For many years, I worked as a professional driver. I saw many friends and coworkers die from "natural causes," i.e., their jobs. Heart attacks, cigarettes, drugs, car crashes, alcoholism, diet, random gunfire, diabetes, cancers... Their jobs killed them every time."

The prodigious Mr. Zackel has published more than a hundred stories, poems, and essays, including a dozen or so novels. Some of his writing may be found under the name of James Cabot. This piece was previously published in *The Mississippi Review* (2006). His latest novel, *Johnny Casino,* is available in trade paperback and e-book through Amazon.com..

Also Available from Darkhouse Books:

We've Been Trumped!
A Light-Hearted Look at Life with President Donald Trump

Paperback available via your local bookstore or Amazon.
Ebook available on Kindle, Nook, and Kobo.

Also Available from Darkhouse Books:

Black Coffee
Stories From the Noir Side of Town

Paperback available via your local bookstore or Amazon.
Ebook available on Kindle, Nook, and Kobo.

Also Available from Darkhouse Books:

Stroies From the Near Future

Paperback available via your local bookstore or Amazon.
Ebook available on Kindle, Nook, and Kobo.

Also Available from Darkhouse Books:

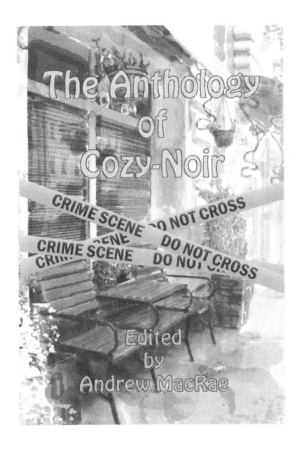

Anthology of Cozy Noir

Paperback available via your local bookstore or Amazon.
Ebook available on Kindle, Nook, and Kobo.

Also Available from Darkhouse Books:

And All Our Yesterdays
Stories of Mystery and Crime Through the Ages

Paperback available via your local bookstore or Amazon.
Ebook available on Kindle, Nook, and Kobo.

Made in the USA
Columbia, SC
02 August 2017